JUST A QUICK NOTE:

Vampire Chained is a M/M vampire romance with on page, spicy sex scenes. If this is not your kind of book then try the Shadow Sentinels Series and the Shadow Sentinels World Standalone Novels. They are all M/F paranormal romance with lots of action and romance, and of course a HEA! (Eventually!)

Elliot and Davlov's novella is set in the same world as the Blood Throne Saga, a new M/M/F spicy romance series.

If you love romance no matter gender, identification, or sexual orientation, then dive into Elliot and Dav's story and have some fun!

Welcome to the world of the Blood Throne Saga!

Join my mailing list for release dates!

For exclusive perks join my PATREON HERE!

Patrons get benefits like raw chapters of my WIP, extra scenes, naming characters, stickers, audio chapters, and much more!

Or my find my AUDIOBOOKS HERE (Subscription)

Twitter
Facebook page

VAMPIRE CHAINED

BOOK DESCRIPTION

I'm an assassin. My first mission? To kill the most powerful Vampire in Europe. What can possibly go wrong?

Entering The Gambit, a sinful supernatural club owned by Count Balthazar Rossi is the last thing I want to do. But I've been imprisoned in a vampire coven all my life, and to escape my stepfather's vicious rule, I'll do anything, even attempt this impossible task.

Inside the club, I don't know where to look. Half-naked demons, deadly fae, sexy shifters, and beautiful Original vampires eye me like I'm dinner. I'm way out of my depth, and I know it.

When my assassination attempt is defeated by the Count's lethal and sexy second in command, I know my life is forfeit.

Davlov Zoltar is powerful, dangerous, and drop-dead gorgeous. Exactly the type who pushes all my buttons. The problem? I'm the lowest of the low, a half-blood human. And he's an Original vampire—my enemy.

When I find myself chained to his wall, I'll do whatever it takes to escape with my life. Except, even as his prisoner, Davlov introduces me to a different world, one where I can be strong and in control.

Discovering my whole life has been a lie shouldn't be a surprise, not when my stepfather treated me worse than a blood slave. Davlov shows me I'm worth far more than I ever believed, and my goal shifts from just surviving, to something far darker.

But can I really leave Davlov behind to reap vengeance when his touch makes not only my blood but my heart and soul, sing?

This standalone M/M vampire novella is set in the dark and seductive world of The Blood Throne Saga where vampires are powerful, sexy, and have no rules about who they play with. Anyone is fair game.

Join Karen's newsletter here for a FREE fantasy book, release news, & writing updates. https://www.karentomlinson.com/reader

Edited by J Soderberg

Cover: Atra Luna Cover & Logo Art

Find more information about Karen's books on
www.karentomlinson.com/books

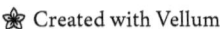 Created with Vellum

lliot

My head snapped to one side, pain exploding through my cheek bone.

Victor grinned, his eyes alight with wicked satisfaction

Straightening my neck and spine, I pressed my lips together, my face blank, just as it always was when I was forced to endure his attention.

Hard eyes scrutinised me. Victor Hamilton was a vampire of the First Order. That meant he was powerful. He was also a sadistic son-of-a-bitch, and my stepfather. His corded muscles rippled as he rolled his shoulders and stretched his neck. He was toned, fit, and covered in a sheen of sweat. I tried not to shrink in on myself. As always his size and strength made me acutely aware of my own physical shortcomings. I dropped my gaze to his booted feet, where the hem of his combat trousers covered the metal bootlace hooks, before raising my gaze to his chest, not his eyes. The fucker was strong and handsome and could charm anyone not clever enough to see the evil beneath. I'd learned long ago to be submissive and act beaten around him. It was a matter of survival.

"Come now, Elee," he drawled, pronouncing my name in such a way as to make it an insult. I hated it. Almost as much as I hated him. "At least try and fight back. It's no fun for me when you don't. Besides, if one day you manage to stop me, maybe I'll keep my promise and clean the human part of your blood." He grabbed my chin and tilted my head, exposing my neck. His sharp thumb nail scraped over my vein. "I could make you a part of this coven, Elee."

Chuckles from his small group of guards filled the air. They fanned the anger I normally locked away. Ever since I hit twenty-five years old, I'd found it harder and harder to swallow down my hatred of my father and his coven. Being part of this coven was all I'd ever wanted. Growing up, I'd believed that it would bring an end to the constant beatings and torment. Now I was older, I realised that if I were to be turned, Victor wouldn't be the one to do it. He'd never agree to it. Still, for some reason I couldn't understand, the little boy in me wanted his approval, to make him proud enough to call me his son and accept me into his beloved circle. I hated myself for it. I both wanted to run from the monster who was the only father I'd ever known, and stay and beg him to love me. It was seriously fucked up considering how clear he'd always made it that he detested me and the very air I breathed.

Victor's mouth twitched at my scowl. He rarely showed any emotion except disgust or disdain when I was around. *Shit!* He'd only torment me more now he knew I wanted to fight back. A quick glance around told me this would end as it always did, only worse. I would be the First Order's punching bag, their amuse-ment for the few minutes it took to beat me until I was unconscious.

Victor struck fast, as only a vampire of his age and power could. I saw the attack, could even project where it would land, but knew nothing I did would prevent it. So did he. My ribs cracked as his heavy boot struck, and I collapsed to my knees. The pain from my chest joined forces with that of my face and my already damaged limbs. I breathed in through my nose, hissing despite trying to hide my agony. There was a lull and I used the reprieve to climb to my feet, leaning forward and holding my ribs. Being a good sport was not Victor's purpose in allowing me to rise. Quite the opposite, in fact. His only purpose was to knock me down again.

From the moment my mother had given birth to me, until now, I'd been the whipping boy for this coven of Made vampires. A familiar anger reached right into my bones. My mother, an Original Vampire, had escaped her mate's cruelty for all of three days before he'd found her and dragged her back to his stately home on the outskirts of Prague. No matter my resentment at her for dying and leaving me here to suffer alone, I had to hand it to my mother, she'd come back pregnant, which from what I'd heard, had saved her life—for a while. Victor had believed it was his. It was only when she'd pushed me out that Victor discovered I was half-human. That was when he'd killed her in a fit of rage. And every day for the past twenty-five years I'd paid for my mother's transgression. When I was five, I'd asked Victor why he hurt me everyday. His response was since he could no longer punish my mother, he would punish me until he decided to kill me.

Being only half-vampire made me too weak to be a competent fighter, and my mixed blood was no use as nutrition either. I was nothing. The lowest of the low in this world of vampires and human slaves. When I'd hit puberty, a newly Made vampire had become obsessed with me and bitten me against my will. I'd laughed until tears ran down my cheeks when he'd projectile vomited all over the floor. Apparently, I tasted sour, and I'd made that fucker ill for days. Of course, Victor had punished me, not the fledgling vampire. Still, at least I'd been spared their fangs, if nothing else, all these years.

A phone trilled from across the room, vibrating against the

top of an old oak writing bureau. Victor frowned and turned away without a second thought, his powerful body eating up the space in no time. Impatiently, he picked it up, but his voice changed the moment he answered it. It was his superior. I had no idea who was more powerful than Victor, and I didn't want to know. At least that phone call meant he'd be distracted.

Relieved, I started to limp away.

"Briony! Keep him there, I'm not done with him yet."

Briony, a tall, elegant woman with a flawless face and long auburn hair smiled coldly. "You heard him, stay there, *ass—assin*."

I ground my molars and ignored the insult in her address. Victor had made Serge, the First Order's combat tutor, train me to kill with a blade and any other close hand to hand weapon starting at six years old. Of course, all the weapons were locked away when I wasn't training. Over the years, I'd often wanted to kill Victor or one of the First Order, but the rune burned into the skin below my right ear prevented me from harming any of them. Not only that, Victor's compulsion not to run kept me a prisoner in this house. I'd tried burning that damned rune away; I'd even cut it out once, but the witch that put it there was powerful, and it just grew back.

I carefully watched all eight of the vampires who surrounded me, my resentment growing as they stared, their pale blue eyes consumed with loathing. My ribs hurt like a bitch, but I wouldn't show weakness under their scrutiny. I stood as straight as I could, letting my hands hang in a relaxed fashion by my sides. It was best to just steel myself for more punishment. I inhaled slowly and deeply, concentrating on the throbbing ache in my face. Oddly, it helped block out the agony from my ribs. Even my father's voice faded as I readied myself for the next round. I rolled my head and shoulders, stretching them. By the time Victor had ended his call, I was ready. Focusing on his face, I prepared for his attack, softening my knees and balling my fists.

He stopped in front of me and regarded me through

narrowed pale blue eyes, and his brows pulled down. After several beats of silence, he spoke. "You have your first assignment. You are to kill Count Balthazar Rossi."

The collective murmurs of the First Order were the first clue this was not a good thing. My heart slammed against my broken ribs. "An a-assignment?" My stammer wasn't something I could prevent. I might have been trained to kill, but I'd never had to actually do it. Shit, I'd never even left this house, let alone tried to plan an assassination. Fear dragged at me, and for all my determination over the years to somehow get away from my tormentors, my palms were sweating. I knew nothing of the world outside this mansion. No, that wasn't true. I knew enough to survive. I'd prepared as much as possible for the day I could escape. That thought settled into my brain, giving me a modicum of calm, which allowed happiness to surge through me. I'd actually be leaving this mausoleum of a house behind! It was almost impossible to hide my overwhelming joy at casting this place and everything it represented aside, but I concentrated on keeping my breathing regular and my pulse steady. After all, managing my reactions and fooling these sadistic animals was the only bit of control I had in my life.

"If you succeed, our Lord has given permission for you to be made a full vampire. If you fail, I will kill you myself."

I swallowed hard. This could be my chance to belong, to have my father look upon me with something other than hate, to treat me with something other than cruelty. Rather than run away into the unknown to have a better life, I could actually belong...

Confusion clouded my thoughts. Did belonging mean more to me than freedom?

"Yes, father..." I whispered, realising my mistake as soon as the words left my lips. Pain bloomed across my face again.

"I am not your father, you disgusting half-breed," he sneered. "But if by some miracle, you manage to kill the most powerful Original Vampire in Europe, I'll deliver you to our Lord myself and recommend he keep you in his household. If nothing else, it'll get you away from me."

I kept my eyes down. I could live with that. Not only would I become a full vampire, I'd get to live somewhere other than with him.

lliot

The energy of the city thrummed through every cell in my body, and I absorbed it like water after a drought. I'd honestly never felt this level of vitality and excitement, not around me or in me. For the first time ever, I felt truly alive. The sounds, the sights, the smells. It was overwhelming and exciting and terrifying, all at once.

I watched traffic dart around London's streets as I walked among people who rushed by me as if I didn't exist. It amazed me that they were all going somewhere, that they all had a purpose. I'd never had a reason to exist, except to be Victor's vessel for revenge on my mother. High above me, on the wall of the beautiful old building across the street, huge screens lit up the sky, advertising the latest action movie. Below it, on another screen, a gorgeous celebrity peered out at me, rugged and perfect with a bottle of aftershave, enticing me to buy it so I could be as handsome and successful as he was.

I huffed, a bitter smile curling my lips. I'd never owned aftershave in my life. I'd been given the basic toiletries to survive, but there'd never been any luxuries, not for me. I had no money of my own, and my clothes had always been threadbare and ill-fitting. Victor said I didn't need or deserve anything except necessary items, and unless my clothes and shoes were falling apart I didn't get different ones. Only the human blood and sex slaves had it worse than me. Some of them didn't even get clothes.

Self-consciously, I brushed my hands down the new jeans I wore before descending the steps into the underground station. These were the nicest clothes I'd ever owned. Victor had given me a budget to buy decent enough attire that I'd blend in and, when it was time, play my part. He'd lifted his compulsion not to run. I'd almost expected him to send someone with me to make sure that I didn't mess this up, but he and the First Order had been given another mission. They'd departed for Canada before I'd even left the house. Not that I was upset about that. I'd been terrified about leaving Victor's home for the first time ever, but I'd rather be by myself than with a malicious vampire who'd take pleasure in ensuring I failed so they could watch Victor end me. Time by myself was a luxury I'd only ever dreamed of; besides, I'd been fine so far. Since I was young, I'd watched videos and researched information about cities all over the world. My lack of possessions hadn't stopped me from making use of the communal computers during the day while the coven slept.

I selected the train I needed and stepped aboard, proud that I had managed to navigate the crazy London underground system.

Hot air rushed by me as I stepped off the tube. Diesel fumes, body odour, and hot air blasted up my nose as the train revved its engine and pulled away. I moved with the crowd, marvelling at the fact that humans really were like cattle being herded from one spot to another, some of them oblivious to the fact that supernaturals walked among them, others deliberately clinging to ignorance if only to maintain their sanity.

The noise of the screeching trains and people hurt my sensitive ears. My heart raced as the overwhelming stimulation hit me. I really couldn't wait to be back out in the open air again. I wasn't used to this amount of noise or this many people being so close. Even if the energy of the city seemed to be feeding my physical and mental strength, I craved the relative silence of the city rooftops where I'd been watching the doors of Count Balthazar's notorious club since I arrived in London a week ago.

I gaped at a male couple who walked past me hand in hand, big smiles on their faces. They looked so happy that my eyes burned. I'd never had that, a partner. I'd had sex plenty in the past. The human's in Victor's house had been as happy to use me as I was to experiment with them, but none of us allowed ourselves the luxury of feelings. That was dangerous ground when humans were expendable and often disappeared. Not once in my life had I experienced any affection. Victor knew no vampire would fuck me, so I'd taken solace where I could, though sex had eventually lost its appeal. My orgasms had stopped pushing away the depressing reality of my life. I'd even given up visiting the human males who were just as desperate to escape their own nightmare as I was.

I scowled and made a fist with my right hand, the cold metal of the ring I wore digging into my fingers. I wasn't here for damned affection, I was here to assassinate the owner of the Gambit nightclub. A move that would gain me a place among the Made vampires and prove that I could be useful as something other than the worthless bastard of an unfaithful Original vampire.

 lliot

Two weeks later, I stared down at the street and released a deep, steadying breath.

"You can do this," I whispered to myself.

The thought of not having to return to Victor's house, of being a fully Made vampire was the only thing forcing my feet to move. I had no idea how a half-human could become a Made, but I guessed it was something to do with the strength of whoever bit me and took my blood. I strode to the rear of the rooftop and jumped, nailing the landing in the alley.

The main street was busy and buzzing with life, as it had been every night. The Gambit didn't shut on any day of the week, not like the other clubs. Its plush glass entrance stood open, welcoming those looking to experience the delights and dangers of a supernatural club. Soft lights enticed, chrome fixtures gleamed, and the sparkling black marble flooring led the way to a night of promise. Off to the left of the main doors, a staircase curved up into the human section of the club. Raucous laughter and excited conversations drifted down, but I turned to the stairs on my right, stairs that led down into the shadows. Power thrummed up from that dark, underground place. It wasn't like anything I'd felt anywhere else in the city. The inky shadows pulsed with that force, brushing my skin, seducing me yet warning me to run.

I didn't run. I wouldn't. I'd been down here before. I was prepared. I'd be fine.

Keeping my head high and my fear locked away, I walked past the huge doormen who supervised both the stairs up to the human club and the ones that led down into the supernatural playground below. Their eyes followed me, their attention like a weight on my back as I disappeared down into the shadows. I knew why; they sensed my human blood. Humans weren't permitted in this part of the club unless they were owned and with their masters or bore the claiming mark of one of the breeds. Even then they were vulnerable. But I'd already discovered my mixed blood gave me a pass.

The soles of my new shoes clicked against the metal steps, the silk mix of my new suit brushing my skin. With each step my breath got shallower and tighter. I wiped my sweaty palms on my thighs, aware of the cameras following my progress. Turning the last corner, my breath hitched, and my heart missed a beat. This wasn't the first time I'd visited the club, but on the previous two occasions I'd tagged along behind another group of Mades. The guards hadn't spared me a glance, not when the group had brought enthralled humans along with them, too.

Tonight, I was alone. I'd seen the Count's Landrover, driven by his second in command, come zooming past. The car had disappeared into the underground garage a couple of hours ago and hadn't resurfaced. A glimpse of tied back blonde hair, a strong profile, and thick corded forearms that led to capable fingers gripping the wheel with surety had burned into my brain. The Count's second was a gorgeous male, yet even from a distance I'd felt the danger radiating from that vehicle like a brush of arctic air on my skin.

I'd used the new phone Victor had given me to do some research, breaking into a cold sweat when I'd realised how powerful the Count really was. But that research had also given me the information I'd needed to get into this club and observe the ancient vampire as well as the guards he stationed around the place. Even the mortal tabloids had images of him and his second in command, Davlov Zoltar, gracing their glossy pages.

I still wondered why Victor had entrusted me with this job. Ending the most powerful Original vampire lord in Europe was a kill order for an experienced assassin, not a nobody like me. Although technically, it hadn't been him that had ordered the hit, had it? It had been our mysterious leader. A vampire who ruled the Mades but had never shown his face in the mansion. I expect Victor knew who it was, but no one else seemed to.

The raucous sound of people having fun reached me from deeper in the dim stairwell. Goosebumps rose on my skin as the darkness pushed against me, testing me, seeing what I was. Runes graced the walls, their magic deciding whether I was the right kind of clientele for this place; well, that and whoever watched the security cameras that followed my progress.

I swallowed against my dry throat. Vampires were beings I should be used to, but I wasn't. Not this kind. I'd discovered that Mades were nowhere near as powerful as blood-born vampires, or Originals as they were known. And Mades had been beating my ass all of my life. Shit, could I really do this? Was I strong enough? My plan was simple, but damned dangerous, and it relied on my powers of seduction. I huffed at myself. Jesus fuck, I was doomed. I never seduced anyone in my damned life.

Two more guards protected the rune covered door to the club, their eyes assessing, their bodies ready to burst into movement if they deemed me a threat.

I exhaled. It was okay. I could do this, I knew how to get past these guys. They just needed to believe I was totally harmless. Sadly, it wasn't hard for me to look that way. I was thin, and even though I was six feet tall, my low body weight made me look younger than I was. And weak. I slumped my shoulders and lowered my eyes, only flicking them up to look briefly at the first guard's face, before lowering my gaze to the ground at his feet.

"Where you going, kid? No humans allowed in here."

"I'm not human, not completely," I explained. Another flicker to his face. "I'm half vampire, and I need in."

A look of disgust crossed his face at my admission.

Yeah, I guessed even Originals were bigoted sons-of-bitches. They still thought a half-blood was a pathetic and disgusting creature, just like my father did. I resisted rolling my eyes. Supernaturals were all beautiful in their own way. That didn't mean they had any more brains than a human.

The other guard chuckled. "Let him in, he's harmless. He's been in before and not caused any problems. Besides, maybe he'll get up enough courage to feed and fuck tonight." His gaze raked from my head down to my toes, his beautiful mouth stretching into a grin. "He's fuckable enough, but looks like he needs a good feeding. Or maybe he'll make a good meal for someone."

"Yeah, it's your funeral, kid," said the first guard.

They both laughed. I ignored them, keeping my gaze fixed on the door as it opened and the smells of the club hit me. Sex, alcohol, sweat, fear, lust, it all mingled in a heady and exhilarating mix. After a pat-down by a handsy female demon, I was in.

Hot bodies pushed against me as I fought my way to the bar. Across the room the fight ring was in full flow. Blood splattered across the floor, and the crowd hissed and cheered. Drinks flowed, and all kinds of species moved seductively against each other. It was packed. It always was. The place was a neutral ground for supernaturals, even with the Made vampires waging war against the Originals—like my mark.

I spied the object of my thoughts. It wasn't hard. The Count sat on his throne like the fucking king of all he surveyed, his dark hair hanging down his back, his bespoke suit clinging to his muscular yet sleek frame. Diamond cufflinks glinted as he moved, almost as lustrous as his stunning, almost colourless eyes.

He oozed power, and shadows slithered around his chair as he moved. Using a firm hand, he yanked the rune-covered, bald-headed witch that he kept at his feet closer by the chain around her neck.

Fear flickered through me. Would that be me by the end of the night? She was clearly his prisoner. What had she done to deserve his wrath? A chill settled in my stomach. What had he done to deserve mine? I felt no hate towards him, no need for vengeance or blood shed. Shit, what the fuck was I doing here? He was my father's enemy, not mine. My heart began racing, confusion clouding my resolve. Could I really do this? Murder someone in cold-blood? Even if I could, the Count was powerful. And I was...definitely not.

As if feeling the weight of my scrutiny he glanced my way, his eyes glittering dangerously. Menace, and the promise of violence far beyond my understanding, glinted in their depths. I tore my gaze away. "Shit..." I murmured, trying to stop my hands shaking. In an effort to calm my anxiety, I sat on a stool, waiting to catch the attention of the barmaid. I needed some kind of courage boost.

"Brandy, please," I requested when she briefly met my gaze.

The pretty blonde nodded before looking down again. I frowned. I wanted to tell her to lift her gaze, that she didn't need to be submissive to me. Gods, I'd spent so long being like her. Weak. Submissive. A target. It made me angry on her behalf. A scarf covered her neck. It didn't take a genius to know what was under it. Scars. Scars that I'd seen so many blood-slaves carry.

At least she looked at me again before taking my money. Pissed-off at the cruelty of this world, I grabbed the glass and knocked back a good mouthful. I didn't like the taste of alcohol, never had, but I enjoyed the burn of the amber liquid as it slipped down my throat, soothing my nerves and giving me the courage I so desperately needed.

Having enough money and freedom to order a drink was still strange, but reality was a bitch. *It's only temporary*, it whispered in my ear. Even if I succeeded, Victor would have to be the one to take me to our Vampire Lord. Having to see Victor again was a fact I hated. It was even worse that I'd have to rely on him to actually keep his word. My eyes flicked back across the sea of heads to the Count. That was if I lived through this...

I knocked back the rest of my drink. Did I really want to become a Made? I was part Original vampire but it was such a weak part of me I might as well be completely human. The thought of being like Victor sent disgust through me, but there was a constant desire in my heart to belong somewhere, and I desperately wanted to believe that my life could be different. Deep down, though, I suspected no matter what happened here, it wouldn't change. I didn't trust Victor to keep his word, but if I ran, he would hunt me down.

I caught the eye of the shy barmaid again. The lights at the far end of the bar illuminated her face. Gods, she looked even more human than me. I was about to order another drink when a deep voice resonated through me, warm breath fanning my ear.

"You want another?"

 avlov

Watching the beautiful young man was no hardship. He was even more stunning in the flesh than he'd looked on the security monitors. He was painfully thin and wearing a cheap suit that was ill-fitting, but there was something about him that called to me. A strange tight feeling invaded my belly as I took in his pretty face. My cock jumped as he tipped the glass of brandy against his soft lips and the slim column of his throat bobbed as he swallowed. I wondered what it would feel like to have those full dusky pink lips wrapped around my cock.

I frowned, grinding my teeth together. No one had stirred this kind of desire in me for so long it was unsettling. Something tugged behind my ribs, a feeling that couldn't be ignored. My heart jumped and raced as I prowled up behind him, quiet and lethal in my movements. I inhaled, his heady scent drifting up my nose. It wasn't a scent I could put my finger on, but something unique, something I knew I'd never forget, not now it was burned into my brain.

I shook my head, utterly thrown by my reaction to him. Was he a witch? Someone sent here by our enemy to bring me down before attacking the Count?

I snarled quietly. The people around me stepped away immediately, but not him. The innocent human was oblivious to the danger at his back. My blood ran colder than ice when he glanced over at my Lord—again. My brain fired warning signals. He seemed to have an unhealthy obsession with the only vampire in this world I was loyal to. Count Balthazar Rossi was my Lord and my best friend. He had been for hundreds of years. Lovers, friends, enemies, they all came and went, but my loyalty to him never wavered and never would. I'd give my very long life for him in the blink of an eye.

Leaning my big body forward, I placed a hand either side of the young man. The bar's surface was so sticky with old alcohol my hands stuck to it. It disgusted me, but I didn't move. Instead, I revelled in his sudden intake of breath and the tremor that ran through him when he realised he was trapped.

"You want another?" I whispered in his ear.

It took mere seconds for his predicament to register, and while it did, I enjoyed the scent of his fear—and the heady aroma of lust. He liked being under my control—or at least what it promised. I'd had years to study and analyse behaviours in all species, and someone like him screamed of submission.

He tilted his head to look at me. I smiled, enjoying his frustration when he couldn't see my face. He tried to push back to see me, except my shoulder prevented him. "Relax, I'm just buying you a drink. I'll not hurt you. Sorcha? Two double brandies."

I held myself there, and he remained still. Gods, my cock was so hard it pushed painfully against my zipper. I was glad he was sitting on a barstool, and I was tall enough to box him in without actually touching his body. That evidence of my desire was a weakness no one needed to know about. I was Davlov Zoltar, right hand to the most powerful vampire lord in Europe. I was a cold and calculating bastard who showed no emotion and would rip out the throat of anyone who threatened the Count or those under his protection.

I ignored the tug on my chest, the one that pulled me closer to the young man, urging me to take what was mine. That deep yearning had gotten worse each time this beautiful man came into the club, pretending to be with a group only to veer far away from them as soon as he could. Watching him on the security system had only fired my need to find out more. He'd turned my emotions into an uncontrollable tempest without him even knowing I existed. I was totally thrown, but I was also intrigued. He was far too interested in my Lord, although that could be because he was just overawed by the powerful allure of the Count. Either way, I needed to know why he was in the Gambit. And I needed to know what spell he'd cast that he could so easily ensnare me.

"If you're buying me a drink, then at least let me see your face." His voice was slightly husky. I hid a smile. It wavered, a slight tang in the air giving away his anxiety. My proximity scared him, but the slight flush to his pale cheeks told me liked it, too. Despite the fact that I never hit on patrons, nor did I accept drinks from anyone, I yanked a stool closer with my foot and perched on it, giving him some space.

We stared at each other, tension and desire thickening the air, sending goosebumps along my arms. His cerulean eyes were the clearest I'd ever seen. I could look at them forever and never get tired of it. Internally, I rolled my eyes. Godsdamn, I was going soft.

Shaking myself, I took in his brown wavy hair and pale skin. His nose was broken, but that didn't detract from his beauty. His lips were full and pouty and begged to be kissed...my breath hitched...and bitten. The thought of sucking that plump softness between my lips and tasting his blood as he moaned my name left me feeling so turned on I had to shift in my seat to hide the evidence of my desire. A small snarl bared my fangs. My reaction was ridiculous. I'd just met the guy, and instinct told me he was here for much more than a quick fuck.

"Here you go, Dav." Sorcha gave me a timid smile and went back to serving. The guard I'd allocated to her watched the customers closely. None of them bothered her, his presence at her back a huge deterrent. So was the scent of the Count, which rolled off her in waves. It alerted all the dangerous and seductive fuckers in here that she was the Count's property. That meant if they tried to harm her they would die, painfully.

I nudged one of the glasses towards the young man. His pupils enlarged as he looked at me, but I forced myself to see past my lust to the man beneath. The scent of fear hit me, yanking me from the fantasy of slamming my mouth against his. Gods, not only was he far younger than the men I usually fucked, he was part human. That meant breakable, but apparently, that didn't seem to matter to my body because I could barely keep from touching him. I fisted my hands, my nails growing and digging into my palms. He affected me like no one else ever had. Made me want things that I'd never had. Dangerous things that had no business entering my head. *Mate. Mine.* I shook those disturbing thoughts away and inhaled again.

"You're vampire...and human?" Involuntarily my lip curled. I hadn't considered that he could actually be a Made. As a hybrid he didn't have the pale blue eyes of one, but it was impossible to tell without tasting his blood. I narrowed my gaze on his face, trying to figure out his deal.

Made vampires had started a bloody and violent war with us, using the human race as weapons. Mades were the undead, humans who were turned into immortals by an Original Vampire. They were once our familiars, humans who had been gifted immortality and served the most ancient families. But that immortality had eventually corrupted even the most loyal of them. The desire to hoard more money, more power, more everything was a hard bitch to tame. The Made Lords had become greedier until it was a corruption that fouled their blood.

That corruption had infected a whole new generation of vampires who were utterly determined to wipe out the Original vampire race. Their ultimate goal was to seize the Blood Throne from the Vampire King and give themselves power over all vampires.

Somehow, the bastards had managed to develop a virus, one that could infect newly Made vampires. Those fledglings became raging monsters with a bloodlust so deep it consumed them. Once it took hold, there was no controlling it. They killed indiscriminately. That virus had started a war that would alienate all vampires from the human race, and potentially destroy any alliances we had with the shifters, fae and demons of this world.

The target of my attention and desire clenched his jaw, his fear turning to something else. Disgust? Disappointment? Anger? It was hard to tell. He shoved the drink back at me, sending it sloshing over the sides, and pushed off his stool.

"Keep your damned drink," he growled and walked off into the crowd.

Snarling, I resisted my instinct to go after him. My fangs grew as I fought the need to shove him up against the wall, slam my body against his, sink my fangs into his neck, and suck until he was screaming my name. It wasn't until my nails scratched deep grooves in the bar that I realised how far gone I was. Shit! I needed to feed, maybe even fuck. It had been a long time since I'd indulged in either. Yup, I was running on empty. I needed blood, that's all this was.

Liar!

No. I shook my head. Not a lie. My self-imposed dry spell had gone on too long.

Scanning the room to make sure the Count was where he should be and that he was safe, I grunted. Two of my men stood behind him. I quickly surveyed the club, ensuring all of the other guards were in place and carefully paying attention to the room. Since the blood war had started, this club had been a powder keg waiting to erupt. It was the Count's territory, one he controlled and defended with an iron fist. His rules were absolute. And I was his iron fist—unless he had a particular reason to dole out the punishments himself.

My gaze snagged on the poor bastards who danced and fucked while chained to several floor to ceiling silver poles. They were enemies who'd betrayed the Count in some way, and he'd let them live. His mercy wasn't always a good thing. Now they were his prisoners, compelled to dance and not stop unless he willed it. They were naked and exposed and could be bought for entertainment. By human standards, it was barbaric retribution, but the supernatural world, and the monsters like me who inhabited it, didn't follow human rules. We had our own justice and punishments.

I looked away, pretending to myself that I wasn't really searching for a beautiful stranger with a head of brown curls. My heart missed a beat when I found him near the fight ring. His eyes met mine, and any anger that he'd had before seemed to have melted away because he blushed under the weight of my stare. Jesus, he was killing me. Need slammed into me. He looked so fucking innocent, so ripe and ready for the taking...

"Fuck it," I muttered and strode through the crowd with purpose, not once breaking that bright blue stare. A small smile curled those kissable lips, and I sped up, that ache in my chest almost stealing my breath. I had to get to him before someone else stole him from me. I'd kill them if they tried!

The fact that I was being irrational, and knew it, didn't matter. I couldn't stop. That feral urge to possess and protect wasn't something I could control any more than I could stop my feet from heading his way.

Within seconds I towered over him. He looked so fragile compared to me, yet there was something in his eyes, a darkness that told me had seen too much pain already in his short life. I lifted my hand and brushed a finger down his cheek. I marvelled at its softness and warmth. He flinched a little.

"Cold," he whispered, his pupils almost swallowing the deep blue of his eyes.

I tilted my head. An original's skin was often cold if they hadn't fed in a while. They only warmed from the ingestion of blood. Mades were always cold no matter what, which confirmed what his scent already told me; he was a half-breed.

I trailed that same finger over his lips and slowly down his neck to the top button of his shirt. His breathing hitched, and I swear I heard a moan beneath the sultry beat of the music.

Feeling myself harden further, I leaned closer. "And you're so warm. Don't worry my touch will warm when I've fed. But cold can feel really, really good too…"

He swallowed hard, peeking up through his eye lashes at me. "I can't wait."

Warning bells reverberated in my head at his change in attitude, especially as the scent of fear lingered, but I silenced them.

"Come with me," I commanded.

His tremor and the hitch in his heartbeat excited me. Fuck, I'd never needed anyone like I needed to touch him, to take him, to taste his warm blood as it slipped across my tongue and down my throat. I was so focused on having him, on acting on the insistent pull behind my ribs that I did what I'd never done before; I took his hand in mine. Revelling in its warmth, I hid my surprise at the feel of calluses on his palm and fingers. My eyes followed his gaze to where he glanced at my Lord. My heart sank, and my chest tightened. I hoped that I was wrong, but despite his reaction to me, there was no lust in his scent.

Taking a breath, and praying to any deities who were listening, I led him through the crowd. Shadows flickered through the air around us, energy licking along my skin. The Count's power was darkness itself. It moved seamlessly through the air, touching, searching and assessing. It was barely noticeable to me after all these years, but the young man's sharp inhale told me he'd felt nothing like it before.

The Count watched us approach, no expression whatsoever

on his face, but I knew him well. His eyes flickered. Yeah, this was way out of character for me, but I had to know...

"Davlov?" he greeted me, a slight frown pulling his black eyebrows low.

"I'm taking an hour," I said, my voice deeper and far more demanding than it should be when talking to my friend and Lord.

The Count's dark gaze moved to the young man who hovered at my side, lingering on the hand clutched tightly in mine.

A low rumble spilt from my lips. A warning. I wasn't letting this man go. Not even for Balthazar. I blinked, common sense yelling that this was insane. The Count could easily rip my head off or the man's if he wished. But no matter the danger, I couldn't and wouldn't let go of my prize.

The Count maintained his relaxed posture, leaning back in his throne with his legs crossed, the picture of suave sophistication and poise. Yet underneath that poise, every being in here knew how deadly he was. Especially me. His gaze focused on my lover-to-be. The man shuffled uneasily, his discomfort sending my protective instincts flaring to life. I wanted to snarl, to show my fangs and warn the Count away from him. Instead, I clamped my lips together, panting heavily through my nostrils.

The Count's intense gaze landed on me. A bead of sweat ran down my temple at his scrutiny. I'd never behaved like this, and though I didn't want to believe what was happening, there was no stopping it. The Count's eyes narrowed, but he calmly nodded, like it was no big deal to see your cold-hearted, hard as fuck, second-in-command meet his mate after hundreds of years.

"Take as long as you need, my friend." Then he uncrossed his legs and uncurled from his chair, stepping close to the man. This time I couldn't help my snarl. Positioning myself between them was instinctual.

Protect... Mine...

The Count's eyes slid smoothly to me, and his large hand landed on my shoulder. "All is well, Dav. I just wish to greet him."

I ground my molars together as he held out his hand to the awestruck young man. My mate stared at it for a second as if unsure whether he should shake it or not. I was aware a number of people were staring, surprise and curiosity on some faces, jealousy on others. The Count was powerful, and alliances with him were constantly sought. They always had been, but he chose his allies sparingly and carefully. What he didn't do was greet strangers by shaking their hand...ever. My heart pounded. Balthazar was the only person I completely trusted. This was my friend's way of telling me he understood my need to be with this stranger, that he recognised the signs of a mating call, even if I wanted to both embrace it and thrust it away harder than I had anything in my life.

The young man's eyes widened at the Count's gesture. A bead of sweat rolled down his temple. I watched it, my instincts screaming something was wrong. A bitter smell hit me at the same time as his fear did. I roared and caught hold of the young man's wrist before the Count could clasp his hand. A ring glinted on the man's middle finger. Just a band of gold metal. Innocuous. Innocent. Until I forced his hand to turn. On the palm side, a tiny spike protruded.

"What the fuck is that?" My grip on his wrist tightened. He whimpered. I was hurting him, but I didn't care. Gods damn him to hell, he'd tried to kill my friend, and he'd used me to do it. Self-disgust rolled through me. I was Bal's best friend and personal bodyguard, and I'd let a pretty face and lust blind me to the danger he was in.

My fangs lengthened and I prepared to rip the man's throat out. Yet as I looked into his frightened eyes, his fear sour in the air, that tug behind my ribs pulsed and I couldn't do it.

"P-Please, don't. I-I..."

Unperturbed, the Count stepped forward, his hand resting on my shoulder. "No, Dav, he lives, for now. Look at me," he quietly commanded the assassin.

The Count's power wasn't something any human, or part

human, could hope to ignore; they were too weak minded to resist. It even washed over me like a cool cloud, soothing my anger, and lending me a calmness that I knew was an illusion. My friend was pushing my anger and guilt aside on purpose. He'd spotted the signs of a fledgling mate bond and knew killing this pathetic excuse for an assassin would hurt me. I took several deep breaths and pulled myself together. This human-vampire reject was nothing to me. I could ignore the hand of fate telling me this was my soulmate. I had to. He was just a stranger, an assassin sent to take out my oldest friend. He didn't deserve anything from me.

Bal's eyes glowed red, his voice soft. "You will not fight, or try to escape. And you will do whatever this male tells you to do." He gestured to me. "Understood?"

The assassin's eyes widened. A vacant look settled on his face before he shook it off and snarled a little.

I looked away. This was the safest course of action, but it didn't mean I had to like my friend having control over this beautiful half-breed. A growl rumbled in my chest as my instincts to yank him away kicked in. What the fuck was wrong with me? He'd just tried to kill Balthazar Rossi! He was either really stupid, or had a death wish.

"What's your name, young one?" asked the Count, utterly cool and in control.

The assassin gritted his teeth and shook his head, his gaze flitting to my mine. He didn't have to answer the Count's question, not when Balthazar had relinquished his compulsion to me. It was clear the youngling hybrid knew what compulsion was, and he was trying like hell to fight it. If Balthazar had to use more compulsion, it could easily break the man's mind and leave him nothing more than a thrall, a slave to whatever my Lord wanted. I glanced over at the silver poles where the Count's other captives danced, touching themselves and being touched by others. I couldn't let that happen.

"Answer him!" I barked, anxiety making my voice harsh.

The man jumped, his gaze flying to mine. His thin body trembled. Whether with rage or fear, I didn't know.

"E-Elliott," he bit out.

The Count nodded. "Thank you, Elliot. Give me that ring."

Elliot just glared, his jaw muscles clenching and his chin lifting. The Count sighed, glancing at me even as my blood sang at the man's courage and defiance of my best friend. Bal could compel him easily, but for some reason had given me that power. And fuck me, if I didn't want to keep it.

"Davlov."

Right. "Take that fucking ring off and give it to him."

Elliot's eyes sparked. I glared back and raised my brows. Elliot swore and continued swearing as he pulled the ring off. Yeah, he could fight it, but in the end he had no choice but to do what I said.

"You will go with Davlov now." The Count looked at me, his pale, almost colourless gaze impassive. "Take the assassin to the castle. Get whatever information you can from him. And use whatever means you think necessary." He narrowed his eyes on Elliot's mutinous face. "I've a feeling that my compulsion will not be permanent, so watch he doesn't try to escape. I will see you in three days. I have business here."

I nodded. "Of course. I will leave a team to protect you and Sorcha."

The Count gave the hint of a smile. "No need. I will see to her safety and mine. Roco will drive me. You take the helicopter back to the castle. Send it back in three days for me."

"Yes, Lord."

"And Davlov?" Bal's gaze was assessing. "Use this time to learn what you need to know about him. While you do, I shall decide whether I will end him for trying to kill me."

I swallowed hard, but nodded. I had no idea how to handle this situation. In all my years on this Earth I'd never met anyone who affected me like Elliot did. In the human world they would laugh at the idea of an instant mate bond, even shifters could have potential mates that weren't necessarily their soulmates. Shifters were lucky if they found their soulmates, their perfect match, but vampires? Original blood-born vampires only had that kind of soul-deep connection with their mate or mates. It wasn't exclusive to other vampires either. A mate bond could be with any race, creed or gender.

"Move." I pushed Elliot forward. His jaw muscles popped as he tried to fight the compulsion, and his face turned red. "Stop fighting the need to do as I say. The more you do, the more painful it becomes."

"Pain won't stop me from breaking your control over me. Or escaping," he mumbled.

I liked his stubbornness, but I doubted he'd be able to break an ancient vampire lord's compulsion that quickly. "Maybe not. But I can tell you now, little human; I will hunt you down and take great pleasure in your punishment." I gave a humourless chuckle as he shuddered. "No? Don't you want me to punish you?"

Elliot shook his head, and I snarled at the intense fear he emitted. He thought I'd hurt him when nothing was further from the truth. Now I realised what that tug was behind my ribs, right into my soul; I wouldn't hurt him, ever. No matter what he did. That didn't mean I wouldn't punish him, though. There were punishments other than pain that could be utter torture. I cleared the thickness in my throat. "Head over there, behind the bar."

Elliot did, his cheap suit somehow looking even bigger on him now, though there was no getting away from his stunning looks. I saw supernaturals checking him out, licking their lips, hunger in their eyes. They wanted him. Fae with lascivious glances and lust burning in their gazes. Demons and shifters with desire in their eyes. Even the Mades watched his progress. They might hate that they were drawn to a hybrid, but it didn't change the fact that they wanted him. There was an air of something light about Elliot that called to the darkness in us all, to our dominant natures. But they wouldn't touch him, not while I was by his side, not unless *they* had a death wish. He was mine. I swallowed hard as something dark and feral buried deep inside me tried to escape.

A fae dressed in a deep grey suit pushed between me and Elliot. Fae were utterly stunning to look at, but just like vampires, their true vicious nature couldn't be totally hidden. Some, like this one, didn't even bother to try. He swept a hand around Elliot's neck, curling it under his jaw. Stepping indecently close, he yanked Elliot close. "Is he to be chained to the poles?" the fae asked, his voice dripping with raw hunger.

Jealousy reared up in me at the sight of that fae touching Elliot's slim neck, his rich chestnut hair gleaming against the fae's pale skin.

A death wish it is, then. "Let go of him now, or I'll rip your arm off."

The fae smiled, his narrowed eyes glinting with challenge. "Hm, I'd love to tussle with you, vampire." He looked me up and down, hunger in his eyes. "I always have. But I also like to play with the Count's enemies. And this one's so soft, so...yielding." His grip tightened on Elliot's neck, and he brushed his semi hard dick against Elliot's thigh.

Elliot winced, and tried to move away. My nostrils flared, anger tearing through me. Only, before I could carry out my threat, Elliot moved. He twisted and speared his fingers into the soft tissues of the fae's neck. The fae gagged and choked, but Elliot wasn't done. He struck hard and fast, shifting his body weight. Another strike connected, his half clenched knuckles spearing into the back of the fae's hand, loosening his hold, before delivering lightning-quick strikes to the other side of the fae's neck. As the fae choked, Elliot spun low, his foot outstretched, and knocked his attacker's legs out from under him. The fae fell heavily, grunting as breath exploded out of his lungs. Elliot swung his leg up, about to smash his heel down on the guy's throat and end him.

Fae were immortals, just like Originals, but just like us, if they weren't powerful enough to heal quickly, they could die from devastating injuries like having your throat crushed by a powerful axe kick.

My insides heated at Elliot's show of strength. Maybe my assassin wasn't so incompetent after all. Feeling an acute sense of pride in his abilities, I grabbed Elliot around his waist and swung him away. His strike landed harmlessly, though I kept my arm around his waist, tightening it as he struggled. Dealing with a dead body wasn't an unusual occurrence in the Gambit, but we'd already drawn enough attention.

"That motherfucker isn't going to treat me like that," Elliot hissed, flicking his hand towards the captive dancers.

I smiled at his rage even though I echoed his sentiments. "You're right. No one is." I let him go. "Go to the door behind the bar. Now."

Elliot glared at me, but didn't fight my command. "Fine," he snapped and marched off. This time everyone gave him a wide berth. I caught the eye of one of my men and gestured at the fallen fae. My man nodded. He'd clean up the mess.

"Where are you taking me?" Elliot asked, the tremble in his voice belying the coldness of his face.

"You don't need to know. Now sleep until I bid you to wake."

"No…" Elliot said, his curls bouncing as he vigorously shook his head.

I raised a brow as he fought the compulsion, his face reddening with effort even as his eyes drooped closed. I caught him as he collapsed and hefted him up over my shoulder. He was too damn light for a male of his height. Well, that wouldn't last. I'd sort that out, just as I'd make sure he was well dressed and cared for better than he ever had been. I gently lowered him into the back seat of the Explorer, fastening a seatbelt across him before jumping into the driver's seat. It was just a short drive to the airport, but a long way back to Scotland, even by helicopter. Still, the thought of having the castle to myself while I got to know this stranger and decided if the mating bond was true actually had warmth spreading through my chest. I rubbed a hand over my heart, unable to comprehend the emotions rolling through me.

I'd never felt so much so fast in my entire six hundred years of life. I glanced back at Elliot, needing to make sure he was comfortable and safe. Gods, he was so fucking beautiful. I had a feeling if he wasn't my soulmate, or if he rejected me, it would break me.

 lliot

"Wake up, assassin."

That deep, sexy voice echoed in my head, forcing me from a fitful slumber. It had been a shitty night as far as sleeping went. I groaned. My arms ached, my shoulders ached. *Everything ached.* I tried to move but found I couldn't. Panic chased the last vestiges of sleep from me. Metal clinked, getting louder with my struggles. I squeezed my eyes shut, realising that I was in a worse position now than I'd been in Victor's home. I'd been a prisoner there, but I'd never been chained. Cold air brushed my skin, pebbling my nipples and raising goose bumps across my naked skin. My feet were bare; only my tight boxers remained.

His deep scent was heavy in the air, curling into my senses. Had he undressed me? The thought was more erotic than it should be considering my position as his prisoner. My huff was soft enough I doubted he'd hear it. It didn't matter. He'd find me disgusting, just as other vampires did. My human blood stopped me from healing as quickly as a vampire, which meant I was badly scarred, covered in welts of puckered pink and white scar tissue. Only my genitals were scar free. I squeezed my eyes more tightly closed, shame burning under my skin. Just once it would be nice to be looked at with something other than revulsion.

"Open your eyes," his deep voice commanded.

The compulsion pulsed through me. There was nothing I could do to refuse Davlov's order. Just like my life before this moment, I was being manipulated and controlled. I opened my eyes and glared at him, anger burning through my chest.

"Let me go."

His smile stole my breath. Gods, he was a handsome bastard. Brown eyes flecked with green glinted in the dim lights of the dungeon. His hair was loose around his face, framing his chiselled jaw.

"No." The smile remained. "But I like that you think you can demand anything from me. It's...cute."

For a moment, I had no idea how to respond. "C-cute?" My growl sounded indignant even to my own ears.

He cocked his head, a gleam in his gaze as he raked it over my half-naked body, lingering on the chains encasing my wrists, arms, lower legs and ankles, before he met my eyes again.

"Yeah, assassin, cute. Here you are chained to a wall. You can't move. You're compelled to do whatever I want, and you still have enough fire to give me orders."

I swallowed hard. His amusement had turned into intense regard, a hungry and feral light in those striking eyes. Suddenly, I didn't feel quite so ugly or disgusting. I felt...desired. Blood sank, making me hard as a rock, and the air became heavy with tension. His eyes widened a bit, and he shifted his position on the chair he straddled, resting his chin on his forearms. His big body stiffened as he inhaled, his gaze dropping to my crotch.

"You like being in chains?" he questioned huskily, his tongue flicking out to lick his lips.

I shivered at the sight, wondering what that tongue would feel like curled around my hard length, teasing and stroking until I climaxed.

My cheeks flushed at my reaction to his question. Did I? Victor had never chained me, though his compulsions and the rune on my skin were still chains of a sort, even if they were invisible. I'd certainly never felt this level of excitement, or this level of lust before. Not when I'd restrained my lovers, not even when I'd been restrained by those who needed the only bit of control they could find as Victor's blood slaves.

I looked my gorgeous and dangerous jailer in the eye. I had nothing to lose by fostering this sexual energy that simmered between us. He was clearly interested in me; I could see it, feel it, even taste his desire. But there was something else pulling me towards him, something that tugged at my chest. I forced that feeling away and gave a sultry smile. I'd felt the heavy weight of Victor's compulsion for years. The Count's was different; lighter, not meant to last. I'd fight it off, and I'd run. Davlov would fuck up eventually, and when he did, I'd be ready.

"Maybe. But I like the way you are looking at me more," I said softly, surprised when I realised my words were true.

His strong throat bobbed. Slowly he stood, a powerhouse of muscle. He wouldn't hurt me. It was in his eyes, in the way his jaw clenched, and the way he wiped his palms on his jeans.

"Tell me who you're working for."

I thought about my answer. The truth was the best option. I was compelled to do what he said, but it didn't mean I couldn't twist my words a bit.

"I have no idea who it is. A powerful vampire."

"Really? You don't know? Then who sent you to end the Count?" I heard the disbelief behind his words.

"I honestly don't know. But a vampire really did send me."

His frustrated growl made me smile. "Okay, clever fucker, tell me everything about yourself. Tell me why you have those scars on your body. Tell me who hurt you," he snapped.

I swallowed, pain reaching into my head as I fought him. I squeezed my eyes shut and roared. "No!"

"You can't fight the compulsion indefinitely, Elliot. Now tell me!" he demanded, his command sending another spike of pain into my head. I panted as I fought the need to tell him everything, clenching and unclenching my teeth until, against my will, the words started to spill from me.

"My name is Elliot, I have no surname, I've no idea who my father was, and my mother was killed after giving birth to me. My stepfather is Victor Hamilton. He's a Made Vampire Lord. He hates me and blames me for my mother's infidelity. He punishes me because I am evidence of her hate and disrespect towards him. She was an Original and he was obsessed with her. He still is. I have no idea if they were fated mates, but their mate bond must have been twisted to shit. He killed her in a fit of rage when he discovered I wasn't his child, that I was a half-breed, a half human piece of shit. He has hated me every day since, and uses me for his amusement. He beats me..." I shrugged, like the physical abuse didn't matter. "You know? Takes his frustrations and anger out on me, as do his warriors, the First Order. I am considered the lowest of the low in his household, even lower than the blood and sex slaves he keeps. I am compelled to stay with him, and this rune..." I turned my head so that he could see it. "Was to stop me from killing any of them. I was trained as an assassin so that I *at least might be of some use*. Those are Victor's words not mine. I'm twenty-five years old, and I had never left the coven until two weeks ago when, out of nowhere, Victor was ordered to send me to kill the Count. He gave me that ring and told me to wear it on my person, that all I needed to do was scratch the Count's skin, and it would eventually poison him." I shook my head in self-disgust, a bitter laugh escaping me. "I couldn't even manage that small task. Not much of an assassin, am I? Now I have no hope of escaping from Victor. I was to be turned into a full vampire upon the completion of my task. Once he knows I have failed, he'll come to kill me, just as he said."

Panting, I fell silent, my eyes clouded with tears, my humiliation complete.

Davlov remained quiet. I understood. There wasn't anything to say. I was such a pathetic creature. He stood, the weight of his stare heavy on my bowed head. His boots clicked on the stone floor until they were all I could see as I sagged against my metal restraints.

"Brace yourself," was the only thing he said before the chains rattled and their tight hold released me. I sank to my knees and stayed there. There was nothing left inside me as the sad reality of my situation hit me. Even if I could escape from here, where would I go?

"Get up, Elliot," Dav said softly, crouching in front of me, close enough that the rumble of his voice touched me deep in my chest. But there was no urgency. He hadn't used compulsion. I blinked as he repeated his words, his breath moved strands of my hair. That tugging on my chest became more forceful, like it was willing me to fight, to prove I was stronger than my despair.

I glanced at Dav's hard yet beautiful face. His jaw was clenched, a furious light in his eyes that I didn't understand. Maybe it was because I hadn't immediately done as he asked. I frowned. I wasn't deliberately defying him, I just didn't see the point in trying. My words made it clear I didn't know anything, that I really was of no use. He'd end me. And a part of me felt relief at not having to fight anymore.

"Get up right now." This time the command in his voice sent a bolt of urgency through me, giving me no choice but to do as he ordered. Once I was up, he gently yet firmly clasped my chin. Holding my gaze, he leaned in, his breath fanning my lips. "You don't ever give up fighting. Not even me. You hear?"

There was no compulsion, just a firm command in his words.

Swallowing hard, I nodded. For some reason, my eyes burned when he nodded back.

"Good. Now follow me."

This time he used compulsion. Involuntarily my feet moved,

and I followed along behind the sleek powerhouse of muscle as he moved smoothly up some ancient winding stone steps that led out into a dark corridor. I tried not to stare at the perfectly shaped, round globes of his arse. Instead, I peered around, hope filtering into my heart. If he wanted me dead, I already would be. And he'd told me to fight. That was an odd thing to demand of a prisoner you were going to kill. That knowledge made me perk up and pay attention.

The stone block construction of the corridor was very old, as was the stone slabbed floor, and the small windows, which were constructed with little diamonds of glass that let in beams of light that danced on the walls.

I was in a damned castle!

I didn't speak, my chest still heavy from the bitter truth of my confessions. My life was such a pitifully sad story. Gods, I'd never even left the walls of the house I'd been born in. How pathetic this ancient vampire must think me.

Davlov led me up a huge wooden staircase and onto another floor. We passed several old doors that must have been bedrooms before he led me up another smaller staircase. There were fewer doors up here, but it didn't smell damp or unused. Nor did it smell of blood and fear like the top floor of Victor's house.

Davlov reached out and opened up a room, gesturing for me to go inside. It wasn't a spoken order, but I was too weary to fight him.

A horrible thought hit me. Perhaps Originals didn't have the same disgust for half-breed blood. Was I to be a blood slave from now on? Terror made my legs shake, but I fought not to let it show.

His eyes bored into the side of my face as I passed him.

"The bathroom's through there. Remember if you try to run, the pain will render you unconscious," he warned. "Go and shower while I find you some suitable clothing. Wait in this room when you're done."

Without another look at him, I stepped into the bathroom

and closed the door. I shucked off my boxers and looked around. It was a luxurious bathroom, modern, clean, and gloriously warm. I swallowed hard, trying to blink away the burn in my eyes. I'd had to use the bathroom shared by the blood slaves. It had been cold, draughty, and old, with no warm water. I'd never been allowed to use a room like this one.

"There are towels in the cupboard, and disposable razors and toothbrushes in the drawers. Help yourself to anything else you need."

I jumped at Davlov's deep voice, nodding, though he couldn't see me through the closed door.

"Thank you," I bit out on a quiet sob.

No one had ever treated me with such respect, and I was his fucking prisoner. What would he treat his lovers like if this was how he treated his enemies?

There was a large walk in shower, which took me a minute to figure out how to work. I stepped under the hot spray and sighed, feeling my muscles unknot as the tension ebbed from them. Stacked neatly on a built-in shelf were bottles of shampoo and body wash. I picked one up and sniffed. The dark and spicy scent was definitely one Davlov used. That thought heated my whole body. I'd smell like him...like I belonged to him.

I gently rubbed my aching wrists and ankles, hating that I couldn't heal like other vampires, but the memory of the look in Davlov's eyes as he asked me if I liked being chained made me ache. I groaned, fisting my hard cock and squeezing it tight. I couldn't lust after my jailer. Not when he would eventually tire of me, then kill me. Desire turned to fear, killing my erection.

Biting my bottom lip, I switched off the water and stepped out, grabbing a large towel from the shelf and drying myself quickly. I frowned at his razor, and the toothbrush in the holder. The thought of a big bad vampire brushing his fangs made me chuckle, but then I sobered.

Oh, gods, this was *his* bathroom. Why was I in his bathroom instead of a guest one?

KAREN TOMLINSON

My stomach tensed. Was he going to force me to become a sex slave? I swallowed hard. I'd always been something other vampires wouldn't touch. Was Davlov different? He desired me, that much was clear, but would he act on it? Did I want him to?

Unwilling to overthink it. I wrapped the towel around my waist and went back into the bedroom.

avlov

Just as I clicked the bedroom door shut behind me, steam laced with the mixed scent of Elliot, and me, came billowing out of the bathroom, followed by the most beautiful man I'd ever seen. And I'd seen plenty over my lifetime. I was as old as sin, yet nothing had ever affected me like the sight of his steam slick body. His short auburn waves gleamed, damp and finger combed back from his face like a silken halo. His face was pink with heat, the flush creeping down his neck, and his eyes were bright. I swallowed hard. Was that how he'd look when he'd just been fucked? All flushed and sexy?

I raked a hand through my hair and cleared my throat, unable to ignore the need that slammed through me. I gripped hard to the sweats and t-shirt I'd found for him, my nails growing, my gaze travelling over the glistening skin of his chest, across his defined abs to the slim V that led under his towel. But it wasn't lust that made me frown. Fury lit a fire in my soul, one that had me itching to hunt down and rip apart every single person who'd ever hurt him. He was covered in marks both old and new, and they went below where the waistband of his boxers had hidden them. Scars that stood prominently on his skin, following the contours of his lean muscles as they crossed the dark trail of hair leading below his low slung towel. I'd missed many of the scars in the gloom of the dungeon. He was thin, too thin, but I already knew that. Yet none of it detracted from his beauty.

Fuck me, he was stunning.

Blood rushed to my face, and I knew I was staring, but I couldn't seem to stop.

"...Dav!"

My attention snapped from the dusky pink skin of his nipples up to his face. He looked amused. Shit, he'd called my name several times by the look of it. And I'd been eye fucking him, all while planning a way to kill the vampires who'd left those fucking scars.

I lowered the bundle of clothes, trying to hide the evidence of his effect on me.

"Um, that's some long claws you're rockin' there, jailer," he said, breaking the tension as we eyed each other warily.

I exhaled heavily, forcing my shoulders down from around my ears. Godsdammit, this young half-breed was tying me in knots. Me, Davlov Zoltar, ancient vampire, personal guard, right hand man, and friend to one of the most powerful vampires in the world.

I couldn't help my gaze straying to Elliot's neck, where I could hear his blood pumping. I wondered how he'd taste, what it would feel like to sink my fangs into that soft flesh and feel the warm saltiness of his blood slipping down my throat until we both climaxed from the sheer pleasure of it.

I blinked hard, my face heating more—along with the rest of my body. I bit my bottom lip, almost groaning at the ache in my engorged cock. Shit. Was it obvious why I was keeping that small bundle of clothes in front of my groin? I had to get out of here or

I was going to make an utter fool of myself. But what he called me bothered me more than my erection did.

"My name is Davlov, or Dav, whichever you prefer, but not jailer."

He cocked a brow. "I did use your name—just—but you were, um, distracted. Besides, you *are* my jailer. I'm not free to leave."

Shit, he was right, he had used my name. Jesus, I needed to pull myself together! I wanted to deny I was his jailer, not only to him but to myself. Wanting him to be here because he'd chosen it, didn't make it so. He was here because he'd tried to end my Lord, and had used my obvious attraction to get closer to his target.

I blinked. In the end, though, even that heinous crime didn't matter. I had to find out if he was my mate—and I only had three days to do it.

"That's true, you aren't. But you can either make your time here pleasant." I shrugged. "Or extremely unpleasant. Either way, you'll be staying with me until I think you're safe to have around my Lord, or until he kills you."

Any amusement dropped from Elliot's face. "Are you going to force me to have sex with you?"

"No, I'm not." Now it was my turn to raise a brow and look amused, even if I wasn't, not one little bit. "I don't need to force anyone. Not to fuck them, or be fucked by them, Elliot."

His face reddened at my words. "Then why am I here? Why not just kill me?"

"Good question, but not one I can answer yet. And I can't kill you."

"Why not?"

"Because, as I said, he wants to kill you himself if you don't give us what we need."

He paled. I hated what that threat did to him, but it was the truth. I couldn't stop Balthazar if he decided death was what Elliot deserved. Volunteering that Elliot was possibly my mate wasn't something I was willing to do at that moment.

"Then why do any of this?" Elliot gestured to the room and

the clothes I still clutched. "What's the point in giving me clothes, or letting me use your room, your things, if I'm just going to be a pet for him until he decides to end me?"

A low growl came from my chest. "You are not his pet!"

In seconds, Elliot was in my face. I didn't move. I didn't want to. He was close enough for me to inhale his clean male scent and see the tiny flecks of darker blue in his irises.

"Then I'm yours," he snapped. "So I'll ask again, what the fuck are you going to do to me if you aren't going to kill me or fuck me, yet I'm in your godsdamn room?"

He wasn't that much shorter than me, but he was far lighter, and I had hundreds of years of training behind me, plus I was of a pure Original bloodline. My strength far outmatched most Original vampires, never mind a half breed human. I grabbed his shoulders and spun him, slamming his back up against the wall. Not hard enough to hurt, but enough to show him who was in charge.

"You seem very preoccupied with me fucking you, Elliot." I ran my nose along his jawline, trailing my lips after in a light touch. "Is that what you want? Tell me."

His breath caught as the compulsion to answer my question kicked in.

"I-I...shit!" His jaw muscles tensed under my lips as he fought his need to answer. "Yes!' He bit out.

I stilled, pulling back enough to look in his eyes, staring at him hard. He didn't look at me, his gaze fixed on the bed. I just wished it was because he wanted us both to be on it right at that moment, but I didn't think it was. He was as attracted to me as I was to him, but he was forced to be here. That made him vulnerable to his emotions—and part of me didn't want him doing what he thought I desired just so I wouldn't hurt him. No, taking him while he was forced to be here wasn't going to happen. But I couldn't give him freedom, or even honesty about what he was to me, not yet. It would leave me vulnerable, and I was too old to put my heart on the line without being sure of him.

I swallowed hard, not used to feeling anything, let alone so damned much. Elliot had gotten under my skin, and there was a real possibility that he would rip my heart right out of my chest. Handling this was the most challenging thing I'd done in years. He had to do as I commanded, at least until the compulsion faded, but I could choose how I spoke to him. I ground my teeth. I wouldn't compel him into giving me information. If he felt safe enough and started to trust me, then he'd give it freely.

I trailed the back of a finger down his cheek, needing to touch him. "Will you look at me?"

He blinked slowly, his nostrils flaring as electricity flared between us. My pulse sped up as he slowly met my eyes. "I want to experience every animalistic, carnal delight, *with* you. But I will never just take it *from* you. That is not who I am."

Elliot's gaze dropped. "Right," he breathed. "People like you don't want me, Dav, and if they do, it's only ever to hurt me."

My own gaze narrowed at his bitter and disbelieving tone, but I shoved my anger at his words away. He had every reason not to trust anyone, including me.

"Yeah, well, I'm different. Don't tar me with the same fucking brush as the people who hurt you. For now…" I stepped away from him. "Get dressed."

He caught the clothes I pushed at him just as his stomach rumbled. That wasn't acceptable.

"Find your way downstairs when you're done. Turn left at the bottom of the main stairs and follow the small corridor to the new wing of the castle. I'll be in the kitchen. We'll eat and then you can accompany me on my rounds of the estate."

Elliot glanced at the window and frowned as if just realising the sun was fully up. "Aren't you a vampire?"

"Of course I am." Where the hell was he going with this line of questioning?

"Then why aren't you behind metal shutters, well away from the sun's rays?"

I blinked. Was he kidding me? But one look at the confusion

on his face, and I knew he wasn't. At that moment, I realised, not only had Elliot been physically abused, he'd been kept ignorant of the vampire world, possibly even the human world.

Careful now, vampire...

The last thing I wanted was to make him think I was ridiculing or lying to him.

"What did the vampires you lived with do in the day?"

"Well, they *slept*. They are nocturnal beings. So why aren't you?"

He was deadly serious. That told me he'd been truthful about being with Mades. Mades were our enemy so sending an innocent like Elliot made sense. As a half-breed, he would be expendable to a Made coven. Elliot might have been trained to kill, but he didn't have the heart for it, the life skills or a wider knowledge of the world. He hadn't been sent as a serious threat, but as a warning. They knew he'd get caught—and likely killed. The ring was a slap in the face to the Count. They were telling us they had the virus and could spread it as they wished, that they would eventually send a true assassin to kill the Count. What they didn't know was how hard he would be to kill, no one but me did.

I just needed to find out which coven Victor Hamilton belonged to. And I would, if only to kill the fucker for what he'd done to Elliot.

"Originals don't need to sleep in the day. Some of us can go out in the daylight. It depends how old and powerful we are. Younglings cannot go out in direct sunlight for hundreds of years. Mades not at all."

"Oh." There was a beat of silence. "So you're really old then?"

I grinned. "Yeah, I'm ancient."

A small smile ticked up the corners of his mouth. "Well, ancient looks good on you." A slight flush coloured his cheeks when I cocked my head and grinned wider.

"Get dressed, Elliot. What would you like to eat?"

"Um, anything," he answered, looking confused.

"No allergies or dislikes then?"

"N-no."

"Good. Omelette it is then. Be downstairs in the kitchen in fifteen." I raised my brows, and lowered the tone of my voice. "Or I'll come looking for you."

I kept the smile off my face. I was close enough to see his pupils dilate as he nodded and moved out of the way, clutching the clothes to his chest as I prowled past him and opened the door.

"Don't keep me waiting," I said for good measure, my voice a little husky as I closed the door behind me.

 lliot

My mouth watered, the aroma of fresh bread leading me down the stairs and along the corridor in the direction Dav had instructed. I swallowed, wondering what bullshit game he was playing. He could make me answer all of his questions in seconds, but he hadn't. I wondered why. Victor wouldn't have hesitated in compelling me. I shuddered. I'd heard the screams of those who resisted his compulsion. Their torture went on for days, sometimes even weeks, before they fell silent. My stepfather was a truly evil bastard. It was strange that, even though I knew he was a toxic presence in my life, I almost wanted to go back to that house. I had to be fucked in the head. Or maybe it was because his rule, and that huge house, was all I'd ever known? My heart lurched. What would I do if I actually got away from here? I had nowhere else to go. I had limited money in my hotel room, no skills to get a job other than killing, and it seemed I was pretty rubbish at that. Even if the Count let me go, Victor would hunt me down.

I lifted my chin and inhaled, Dav's soft command echoing in

my mind. I'd survive, that's what I'd do, if only to spite that evil motherfucker.

The kitchen turned out to be modern and light. Overhead, a glass roof proved what Davlov had said about being immune to sunlight. I frowned. I'd always assumed I could walk in the day because of my human blood, but my mother had been an Original. Had she been old? I didn't know much about her at all, except her first name. No one had ever talked about her, and I'd never dared ask Victor any questions.

My footsteps slowed. Davlov stood with his back to me, a frying pan on the flat black glass hob. On the large island in the centre of the luxury kitchen, there was a breadboard where some fresh bread steamed, the smell making me salivate. I was so hungry... I eyed the bread knife. It would take me only five steps to grab it, and though the blade didn't have a point, I'd be able to do some real damage with it...

"You know, if you keep staring at me like that, I'll think you're either eye fucking me, or about to grab that bread knife to stick in my back."

Despite my circumstances, I smiled. "Nah, I'd not stick in your back. I'd slit your throat."

He chuckled, a deep sound that sank right into my bones. Turning slightly, he slid a perfect cheese and vegetable omelette onto a plate and prowled over to the table. Each step was measured and powerful, making me feel clumsy and so very out of my league as I followed, sitting where he indicated.

"Eat while it's hot. And eat plenty. You'll be by my side while I go and check in with my guards. Then we'll walk the perimeter wall and check the runes that protect it."

I nearly choked on the piece of bread I'd just bitten into. "You're taking me and showing me your defences? Isn't that a bit stupid?"

"Nope, because you won't know what the runes mean or how to use them, and until I trust you, you aren't leaving my side."

Dav's grin did funny things to my insides until his words registered.

I swallowed, the bread getting stuck in my throat. "Or the Count ends me?"

Dav's grin fell. "Something like that."

I pushed my fear away. I couldn't escape. Every time the thought entered my head, it floated away as if I couldn't form any thoughts around leaving. I looked at my butter knife, rolling it between my fingers and thumb. I frowned. I didn't want to use it, not to hurt the vampire sitting within striking distance of me. I put it down.

"Eat, Elliot."

While I did, I went over my disastrous attempt at killing someone I'd never had a hope in hell's chance of ending. I wondered why I'd even been sent. It didn't take much to realise Victor had looked so pleased because he knew I'd fail. I'd been a message, that was all. A dispensable asset. I slowly put my knife and fork down.

"What's the matter? Aren't you hungry?"

"They used me didn't they?"

Davlov put his own cutlery down. I stared at his plate. Didn't Originals feed on blood like Mades? I'd always believed they did. But it seemed much of what I'd understood about vampires from Victor was bullshit.

"They did. Your ring has no poison on that sharp spike. If Victor hadn't wanted us to discover you, he wouldn't have mixed the blood on that spike with garlic, which he knew the Count and I would scent."

"Garlic..." I interrupted. "But I thought garlic didn't kill vampires; that it's an old wives tale."

He sighed and met my gaze with a pitying smile. "Whoever told you that was partly right. It won't kill an old Original. It will burn like a bitch, but we can recover. Younglings and Mades can be poisoned by it though."

"Oh." Had Victor told me it was harmless because he'd

thought I'd use it to kill him? Victor had done more than abuse me all these years, he'd lied through his godsdamned fangs.

Awkward silence settled. "Elliot, Victor lied to you. A lot. You were sent here as a message." My fingers rolled into fists as my suspicions were confirmed. "One he knew we'd intercept...and kill."

I nodded and picked up my knife and fork, cold hatred settling in my belly. I'd do whatever it took to survive this. I'd tell Davlov and the Count whatever they wanted. Somehow I'd get back to Victor. And then the man who'd killed my mother, abused me, and sent me away to die, was done. I'd do whatever it took to end the evil bastard. Even if it meant I'd die too.

"Hey, now." A big hand covered mine. "You're bending the cutlery," Davlov cautioned, gently, prying the bent knife and fork from my fingers.

"Sorry," I said, my voice tight.

There was a beat of silence. "Here, use mine. I'm done."

"Thank you, but I'm not hungry anymore. "

I could literally feel his eyes boring into the top of my head from where he sat opposite me.

Ancient power brushed over my skin. "Yes, you are. Now finish it all. If you want revenge you need to build up your physical strength."

My head snapped up. His steady, cold stare held mine. I shivered. A merciless killer stared back at me.

I swallowed, common sense telling me that his wrath wasn't aimed at me, but I couldn't stop that instinctual need to recoil, my breath catching. It wouldn't be long now until the blows fell.

"H-how do you know what I'm thinking?" I asked, my gaze locked on my plate. Maybe if I showed him I was no threat, that my need for revenge wasn't aimed at him, he would at least pull his punches...

His chair squeaked, and gods help me, I couldn't help but flinch. I'd taken so many beatings in my life that I was never surprised by an attack, but expecting it didn't make it hurt any less.

"Because that's what you *should* be thinking about."

Firm fingers gripped my chin, forcing me to look up and meet his now ruby eyes; eyes that promised pain to anyone who crossed him.

"Elliot, I promise you, no matter what you tried to do to the Count, you will not be mistreated, beaten, starved, or used for pleasure while you are in this castle, not by me, or anyone else. You are under my protection." There was a pause. His eyes stayed cold, a slight snarl to his upper lip revealing his fangs.

The sight did something to be. Liquid heat flooded my limbs, and I leaned towards him, unable to take my eyes from his.

"Even from the Count. Do I make myself clear?"

It was impossible to hide my reaction. My throat ached and my eyes stung. No one had ever promised me anything, let alone that they were going to protect me. I couldn't speak, so I nodded. His thumb brushed my lower lip, sending sparks through every cell in my body.

"Good. Now, are you going to eat? You have a long day ahead, and you'll need your strength for what we are going to do."

"Why? What are we going to do?"

He just grinned. "I've already told you."

Somehow I knew he was planning something more than inspecting a perimeter and checking in with his men. I huffed. "Okay, what *else* have you got planned then?"

That shit eating grin just stayed there. "You'll see. Just be warned, I might be awake now, but I prefer the night, so you'd better learn to like it too. You're going to be awake for a long time today. "

I smiled. A part of me was still waiting for the blows to fall, but another part of my brain told me they never would; that I could trust his promise. I cocked my head, softening my voice. "So I sleep when you sleep. Wake when you wake?"

"That's right."

"Then I think I'll learn to like it just fine."

Dav's satisfied smile did something to me, but he didn't say anything else. He just released my chin and looked pointedly at the cutlery he'd passed me. I picked them up and finished every morsel of the omelette. It wasn't hard, my stomach was cramping with hunger. Even since leaving Victor's, no matter how much I ate, I was always starving. It was nothing new. I couldn't remember a time when I'd not been hungry.

While I finished, Dav cleaned up. As soon as I swallowed the last mouthful of that delicious omelette, he took my plate. I watched him move, enjoying the way his t-shirt moulded to the muscles of his torso and his large defined arms as he cleaned the kitchen. My cheeks heated. What would it be like to be held in those arms? To be kissed by that full mouth? Or to feel the strength of his body against mine?

The smooth and powerful way he moved was predatory. He wasn't just a bodyguard, he was a warrior, his body a lethal weapon wrapped in the trappings of civilised life. I smiled to myself, wondering at all the fashions he must have worn over the years. Frills and pantaloons came to mind and I couldn't suppress a snort of laughter at the image of this kickass vampire warrior dressed so ridiculously.

Dav eyed me suspiciously. "What?"

I coughed and cleared my throat, trying to look innocent. "Nothing. Nothing at all."

He narrowed his eyes but went back to wiping down the marble kitchen top.

Happily, I eyed his perfect arse. Nope, it really didn't matter, he'd look hot whatever he wore.

 avlov

Elliot aimed the gun and smoothly pulled the trigger.

"That's it," I whispered in his ear, releasing my hold on his arms.

"Thanks," he said huskily, before he coughed, clearing the hoarseness from his voice.

I smiled. It had been like this for three days. We'd get up early in the evening, and I'd make him eat before I caught up with my men, got a report and planned the security detail for the night.

Even though Elliot ate everything I gave him, I worried about his rapid weight loss. He got tired quickly, and wasn't anywhere near as strong as I'd have expected a part breed vampire to be. I'd ask the Count's permission to get one of our doctors to see him. My urge to make sure he was cared for and not in need of anything wasn't something I could deny.

Some of my men entered the gym. Their faces flickered with surprise at my closeness to the male, who was essentially my prisoner before they masked it and greeted Elliot politely. I bit down on a snarl as Vito, a guard I'd known for at least two hundred years, eyed Elliot up and down before smirking and licking his lips.

Showing them what he meant to me was not an option. They'd tell him why I was so attentive, either by design or mistake, and that wasn't how I wanted Elliot to find out. I wanted him to come to me of his own accord because he was drawn to me and wanted to be with me—but only when he was free and safe. Until the Count returned, not even I could guarantee his safety.

I ushered Elliot over to a matted area. At least, when I threw him, he'd not hurt himself.

"Come on, time to learn some knife defence skills that actually work. Not something some idiot just told you would work when the moves mean nothing against someone far stronger than you."

Elliot's dark brows drew down. We'd discovered that as well as being lied to, his 'training' had been less than stellar. Since we'd started to teach him some effective fighting techniques, he'd progressed more quickly than any recruit we'd had before. He listened, practised and then executed with such skill it amazed even me. He was a natural fighter. With more strength, knowledge, and endurance, he'd be lethal.

I grinned at him as he blocked my simple knife attack and landed a punch in my ribs. He wasn't powerful enough to hurt me, but he would be if he ever unlocked his vampire nature. Maybe constant training, and more self-confidence would make that happen?

"Well done. That was a good, clean attack." I stood tall and smirked. "But let's see what you can do against this knife attack."

And so it went. Elliot and I trained until the early hours of each night. I neglected as many of my duties as I could, hoping to see the compulsion to complete my orders fade. I wanted him to have his free will back. My stomach clenched at the thought that he might never get that chance if Balthazar decided he should die. My nostrils flared. I couldn't let that happen. Elliot had been abused all of his life, coerced and bullied into doing what Victor wanted. He'd been thought of as disposable, a sacrifice to send a message. Surely, the Count would see reason? Especially now. These past few days had cemented my feelings. He was my mate. I knew it. Even if he didn't.

A fist hit my jaw, snapping my head back. Elliot laughed. A sound so joyful and full of pride, it had me chuckling too.

"Oh my gods, I got you! I actually managed to hit you!" he laughed.

I raised a brow and sucked some blood from the tiny split on my lip, trying to make it look worse than it was. Elliot deserved some praise and self-confidence. I doubted the bastard who'd abused him all of his life had ever given him any.

"Yeah, you did. Awesome work. Now do it again." I grinned at his groan.

"But I'm starving!" he complained.

Now I really did laugh. "You're always starving. Ten more minutes, and we'll go and shower. I'll cook you steak, rare, and then you need to go to bed. We both do." The sun was already rising, the blue sky visible through the gym window.

He flushed prettily. Fuck he was beautiful when he was bashful. My fangs lengthened, and I didn't bother to hide them. The thought of letting him go, or worse, of him not being in this world anymore, had my chest tightening so much, I had to tip my head back and take a slow deep breath to calm my panic.

"Dav? Are you okay?"

I met his clear blue gaze. "Of course. Now, come on. If you want that steak, you need to land another punch."

I was aware of my men watching our exchange with curious glances. Ignoring them, I focused on Elliot, and after blocking a few of his attacks, I let him strike me again.

The next day I rose from my half of the bed. I was tired and fucking hungry. Not for food, but for blood. Sleeping with Elliot was torture, but I couldn't bare the thought of him somewhere else. I wanted him by my side, to care for...to love. But resisting the temptation to pull him beneath me and show him how much pleasure his body could take and give was getting harder and harder. I rubbed my eyes then glanced down at his face. Reaching out, I ran my fingers lightly over his messy brown curls. Dark circles marked his eyes.

I hated that sign of worry. Despite my promises to keep him safe, I couldn't reassure him that everything would be okay. At least I had a little longer with him. The Count wasn't returning for another week or more, but that also meant our future was on hold until I convinced Bal that Elliot was my mate and that he could be trusted.

A hand grabbed my wrist. I held back a flush at being caught touching him.

"Morning, jailer." Elliot smiled, his eyelids heavy with sleep, but his smile faltered. "Hey, are you okay?" A small frown pulled at his brows.

"Yeah, I'm fine." *Liar.* I was so messed up, I had no idea how to deal with it.

"Okay, good." He snuggled down under the covers with a cheeky grin baring his white teeth before he turned on his side. "Then you get the shower first, and I get to stay in bed."

Thud...

Thud...

Thud...

I blinked, inhaling sharply at the call of his blood. My cock punched out at the thought of sinking my fangs into his neck and tasting that red nectar. He'd smell of me, *my* scent mixed with his. Everyone would know he was mine... My heart slammed against my ribs, slow like any ancient Original vampire's, but still fucking loud as desire and the need to feed ripped through me.

Before he noticed my predicament, I threw myself out of bed

and marched into the bathroom, thankful he was facing the other way. I just needed to go to the Gambit and feed from fresh warm blood; that would quench this violent thirst.

I stepped into the shower and leaned forward under the spray, my hands flat on the cold tiles.

It wouldn't. And I knew it.

My morning wood throbbed painfully. I was light-headed from blood hunger, but the thought of feeding on anyone other than Elliot filled me with disgust. I was old enough I didn't need to feed often, but taking blood always resulted in an intense orgasm. I shivered and fisted my cock, the thought of experiencing that with Elliot was too much. I worked myself until I shot my load all over the wet wall, gritting my teeth and holding my groan in my throat.

"Jesus," I muttered as I washed away the evidence of my release. This was fucking torture. I needed the Count to come home. Not just for Elliot's sake, but for mine.

The day passed quickly and uneventfully. Elliot's company was a joy. His incessant questioning about the running of the estate; about what being an Original meant, not to mention his reaction to learning we lived indefinitely and that, yes, we could be killed by a stake to the heart or being beheaded; that we had a whole race of Originals that lived on this planet who weren't warriors, but who blended in with human society, was absolutely adorable.

"So why do you fight Victor's kind then?"

"Because the Mades developed the Bloodlust virus and brought the war to us, specifically the Count."

"Why him? Why not the Vampire King?"

"Because he is as powerful as the King and has just as much, if not more, political influence. The King is weak in body and mind, he always has been. His authority is dying among our kind, and our enemies know it. His son is a young boy and not in any position to sit on the Blood Throne and run our kingdom. Whoever sits upon that throne rules our kind, all of our kind,

Original and Made. If they can kill the Count, ending the King's reign will be easy. The Count is the King's strongest ally and advisor. He has connections across the world. Without Balthazar, the King's defences would falter, and whoever is leading the Mades will be in a prime position to take the throne."

Elliot's eyes widened. "Wow," he murmured.

We continued to walk the perimeter wall, but after a few minutes of silence, I'd had enough.

"Hey."

I put a hand on his shoulder and pulled him to a stop before peering into his eyes. "What's going through that busy mind of yours? You've done nothing but pepper me with questions the whole day, yet now I've told you what the war is about—nothing."

He shrugged, but couldn't turn away when I firmly grabbed his chin between my fingers and thumb.

"Not good enough, Elliot." I smirked. "You don't get to be moody around me."

He rolled his eyes, but a sexy little smile curled the corners of his mouth. "No, that's your job."

I grinned. "True. Now tell me what's on your mind."

He tilted his head, his lips pressed firmly together. A sigh escaped him, but there was a determined glint in his eyes. "I can lead you to the general area of Victor's stronghold. His man blindfolded me to drive me to the airport, but I know roughly how long it took, and I know we were near Prague because that's where my flight left from."

"He could have just driven you around to confuse you."

"He could, but even if he did, I can help you search for the coven."

I searched his face. "You really mean that, don't you?"

"I do."

"What about your own revenge on Victor?"

He shrugged. "I think we both know I'd mess it up."

I tightened my grip. "No, I don't think you would. You are stronger than you think, Elliot. You just need to realise it."

I let him go and walked back to the car, waiting for him to catch up when I made it back slightly before him. He looked lost in thought as I turned the key, and he remained silent all the way to the estate's gatehouse.

His silence continued as I checked in with the guards.

"Keep me informed of any issues," I said to Vito, relieved to be almost done. No matter how it tested my self-control, I craved the daytime when I could lay close to Elliot. "The Count informed me of another virus outbreak in South London. He's stayed to do some damage control, but I want every part of this estate warded and locked down."

The guard nodded, then looked intently at Elliot before shifting his gaze back to me.

"Why're you dragging round a half-breed, boss? It's not like you to waste your time training someone as low as him to fight and use weapons when he'll be dead soon." His gaze raked over Elliot, a roguish glint in his eyes. "On second thought, shall I watch him for you? I'll bet his human blood tastes really fucking good."

I snarled and glanced at Elliot, who quickly looked at the ground, shrinking in on himself. Vito was being an arse, trying to wind me up, but in the process he was frightening Elliot. Frustration had me grinding my teeth. Elliot *was* technically my prisoner, and no matter how much I wanted to keep my promise to protect him, I had no hope of defying Bal if he wanted Elliot punished. If I fought my friend to protect Elliot, he'd kill us both. I swallowed hard, hating that for the first time ever I was questioning my loyalty to my friend and Lord, for a bond that was only just forming between me and Elliot. Either way Vito had no understanding of how his words affected Elliot. But he soon would. Elliot had been abused all his life; that wasn't happening anymore—ever.

"Elliot. Go and wait outside."

I had refrained from using any commands recently and his glare told me he realised he couldn't defy this order. I would have been happy at that show of rebellion if he hadn't dropped his gaze when Vito chuckled. I snarled as Elliot curled in on himself and walked out without a word. In the blink of an eye I had Vito around his thick neck and slammed him up against the wall.

"Yeah, he's my prisoner, you arsehole. But he is worth every bit of my time, and anyone else's that I say. Know this. If you ever touch him or disrespect him again, I'll break you. You feel me?" I snarled.

"Whoa, okay, boss." Vito lifted his hands and eyed the door speculatively. "You sure he's your prisoner?"

"Yes!" I snapped.

Vito raised his brows, but shrugged. "So you want me to shoot him if he runs?"

My fangs dropped, long sharp and lethal. I could end one of my own kind. I was one of only a handful of Originals old enough and powerful enough to do that with a bite. "Hurt him and I'll rip your throat out."

Vito had to have a death wish because he just gave me a shit eating grin. "I won't hurt him, boss. He is fucking beautiful to look at. I get it. Really, I do. I'd be *real* nice to him, too, if he was *my* prisoner."

I roared and threw him across the room. The wall cracked as he slammed into it. He half groaned, half laughed as he pushed himself into a sitting position and shook dust from his arms and shoulders. "Godsdamn, Davlov, it's true then. Roco told me you were fucked. I didn't believe him, but, hell's teeth, brother, you really are."

My nostrils flared. "Roco phoned you?"

Vito nodded, groaning as he pushed to his feet. "He saw you at the club. Said he'd never seen you so wrapped up in a piece of arse before."

"That little shit's a worse gossip than any female I've ever met."

Vito snorted. "Yeah, he is. But he's right, isn't he? That pretty mixed blood's your mate, isn't he?"

"Fuck off. He's not." I wasn't admitting that to anyone, least of all the males who looked to me as their commander. If I failed to get Elliot to recognise what we were to each other, and Bal chose to end Elliot's life, none of them needed to know how destroyed I'd be. Fear punched through me. Not for me, but for Elliot. I had to talk to the Count, but my stomach clenched. I knew better than anyone that he was as unforgiving as they came to those who threatened him or the people he considered his family.

"He's a prisoner and that's all."

I stormed out of the building and headed to the SUV that I used around the Estate. Turning the key, I fired up the engine. Elliot climbed into the car, his face dark as he stared forward.

"Put your seatbelt on!" My fingers tightened around the wheel when he panted, trying to defy my order. "Just fucking do it!" I barked, angry that he was causing himself pain.

A growl erupted from his chest, but the click of the belt satisfied me enough to move off. I hit the pedal, and we lurched forward in a spray of gravel. I didn't speak again. I couldn't. I hated that I couldn't act on my feelings, that everyone who knew me could tell how utterly besotted I was, even if I didn't want them to know, while Elliot had no fucking clue. I threw the car around the sharp bends of the estate roads, heading back to the castle. I needed blood, sleep, and some time alone to get my damned head together.

"Slow down!" Elliot yelled when I almost skidded around a bend and he banged his shoulder against the door, his hand shooting out to brace himself. "You might be immortal, but I'm not, you dick!"

I glared at him, baring my fangs, my grip tightening on the steering wheel when I saw how pale he was. *"Fuck!"* I uttered. He'd not been in a car much if he was being honest about not being let out of his previous home. Another self-derisive snarl twisted my mouth. Of course, he'd told me the truth! I'd met liars before, and Elliot wasn't one.

I growled, my grip tightening even more on the wheel. It creaked under my assault.

Not only had I lied about what Elliot was to me, I'd hurt and scared him. Forcing myself to control my emotions, I eased my foot off the pedal, loosened my grip, and drove steadily the rest of the way back. I still braked harder than I meant to, stopping outside the side entrance of the castle in a spray of gravel. Without speaking, I jumped out and strode for the door, unable to deal with being near him until I'd calmed down.

"Hey!" Elliot shouted.

I ignored him, my fists curled, tension about ready to make me smash the nearest wall to dust. Flinging open the door, I marched across the light and airy kitchen, through the dining room and along a long corridor into the gym, slamming the door behind me. A second later the door swung open, banging loudly against the wall.

"You don't get to storm away from me!" he yelled, breathing hard as he marched into my personal space, standing almost nose to nose with me, fury rolling off him. "You'll protect me from everyone, Davlov? How about your own men?"

"I did protect you!" I roared.

"Fuck you! What happens when you're not around? I'm a half-breed, just fresh meat to them!"

"You are mine! My prisoner! They will never hurt you!"

His laugh was cold and bitter. "Yeah? Well, life's taught me different, so fuck you and your godsdamned empty promises!" His nostrils flared, a snarl curling his lips. "I should have known you were no better than Victor. You're both fucking liars!" He spun away, but his words cut deep.

"Where do you think you're going?" I caught his arm and spun him back to me, catching him around his waist and thrusting a hand into his hair, pulling hard until he had to arch back.

"Away from you..."

"You're never getting away from me. Not now, not ever," I growled as I slammed my mouth against his, claiming him in an

61

aggressively rough kiss. He moaned into my mouth, his body melting into my hold. Gods, he destroyed me, his taste, his smell, the feel of his hair gripped in my hand, and especially the way his body softened into my touch. I deepened the kiss, invading his mouth with my tongue, claiming him. Our moans mixed as I lowered him to the soft training mat, the feel of his compliant body under mine shredding my self control. My cock throbbed, aching and jumping with every sound he made. I ground against his hard length until he whimpered, his need clear in the thrust of his pelvis.

I pulled away.

"No…" he whispered, grasping at my forearms.

"I'm not going anywhere," I growled. "But is this really what you want?"

He groaned, looking at where I fisted myself through my combats, trying to ease the ache.

"Yes, gods, yes."

"Good, because that was your chance to say no. You're mine now," I growled, not caring about the possessiveness in my tone. I ripped his shirt open, taking in every part of his creamy skin, every scar and dip of muscle. "Beautiful," I murmured, not missing the disbelief on his face. "You fucking are," I growled, leaning forward to move my lips along his jawline as I worked his arms out of his shirt. His stubble was rough on my lips and tongue, only making me more desperate. I continued my journey down his body, controlling my need to take him, to bite him. Instead, I laved his chest with my tongue, sucking and biting his nipples until he was panting and whimpering my name.

"You like that?" I whispered against his skin.

"Fuck, yes, yes, I like that."

I smiled at the desperation in his voice and lifted myself off his chest, grinding my lower half against his.

"Dav! Please!"

My own chest was heaving, my balls so tight, my cock so hard, if I didn't get inside him soon I'd explode like a fledgling in bloodlust. I sat back and knelt between his legs, utterly transfixed by the sight of his flushed face and bright eyes. My gaze flayed him, taking in every stunning thing about him until his tented sweats snagged my attention.

"I want to see you." My voice was thick with lust. He nodded, and I pulled them off, along with the rest of his clothes. His cock bounced free, mouthwatering, thick, and so fucking hard. I groaned. "Jesus, I need to be inside you."

"Yes. Now," he demanded, leaning forward and gripping my hips.

I snarled and grabbed his hands, pushing them slowly, yet firmly into the floor above his head. "Was that an order?" I purred, holding his gaze..

His eyes widened, and he whimpered, his pupils blown as I held him immobile. Oh, he really liked being restrained. He was a submissive, and my chest warmed with the knowledge that he would already give me enough trust to hold him like that after all he'd been through. I brushed my lips along his jaw and felt his cock pulse against my thigh.

"Is this okay, Elliot?" I asked, squeezing my hold on his wrists tighter.

He nodded.

"Use words. Tell me. I need to know for sure."

"Yes," he breathed. "I-I like it."

"Good." I kissed the corners of his mouth. "Then keep your hands there. This is all about you and your pleasure, not mine."

"O-Okay."

I smiled and held his gaze while I sat back and undid my belt. Gods, I'd never seen anything as exquisite as my mate lying under me, giving me complete control. His trust was a gift I couldn't fathom. Had anyone ever done anything just for him? I doubted it.

"Fuck me, you're stunning," I breathed.

It was true. The sight of him panting with desire, his eyes hooded, unleashed something inside me that I couldn't explain;

something that warmed my cold and ancient heart. At the same time, I knew beyond any doubt that it made me far more dangerous because if someone hurt him, I'd destroy the world and everyone in it to exact my revenge.

He watched, transfixed as I pulled off my shirt before I stood and shed my combats, boxers and boots. His attention dropped to my engorged length and I throbbed, twitching under his intense gaze. Unable to stand the ache any longer, I grabbed my dick and squeezed hard as I dropped down to my knees.

He whimpered, arching his spine as I ran my fingertips slowly from his wrists, down his arms and body, touching and teasing every inch of his skin, except where I knew he most wanted it.

"Dav, please, touch me," he eventually begged, undulating his hips.

I smiled, lust ripping through me. Lowering myself, I dragged my tongue up his engorged length, smiling as he whined and thrust against the air, writhing desperately. But making him wait only tortured me, too. I'd never wanted anyone as badly as I wanted him. I reached for my discarded combats and pulled a packet of lube from my pocket, tearing it open with my teeth and dropping it beside his thigh. His eyes were hooded as he murmured my name. I leaned over him, teasing and touching him with my fingers and mouth, gripping his balls and massaging them but never touching his engorged erection. He started to beg, my name a constant whisper from his lips as he wildly thrust upwards.

I growled and held his hips still, then with a purr I licked the underside of his cock from balls to tip, lapping up the precum leaking from his slit. His taste exploded in my mouth and I couldn't resist any longer. I swallowed him down. Hollowing my cheeks, I sucked hard and slowly pulled back. He yelled my name and satisfaction rolled through me at the pleasure thickening his voice.

I grabbed his thick base with one hand and leaned some weight on his pelvis with the other to prevent his desperate thrusts as I moved on him. Sucking him hard, I slicked my fingers with the lube. Carefully, I slid a finger into his body, humming around his cock as he tightened and pulled me into his heat. I worked him until he was bucking against me, then added another finger, and another, stretching him until I judged he was ready to take me.

I released him from my mouth with a pop but kept my fingers moving inside him.

"No, no, don't stop. I need…"

I lifted my head and held his lust-filled stare, moving my heavy body over him while keeping my fingers moving. "I know what you need, baby. Trust me, Elliot. This body, this cock. They're mine. *You're* mine. And I'm going to fuck you so hard, so good, that you'll know it too. Then I'm going to take you again and again, until you forget your own damned name. Now tell me with words what you want." I hooked my finger forward finding the firmness of his prostate and massaging it, revelling in the gasp that fell from his lips.

"Holy fuck…" Elliot whimpered, his cock jumping under my stomach, his hips moving, desperate for some friction.

"Tell me." There was no resistance at all to my demand, even though I used no compulsion.

"Please, Dav, please…I need to feel you inside me. Take me. Fuck me hard. Please…ohhh…"

Satisfaction rolled through me, and he hadn't finished begging when I moved. Withdrawing my fingers carefully from his body, I knelt. He watched with hooded eyes as I lathered more lube on my swollen length, then hooked his thighs with my arms, opening him to me. I leaned over him, supporting my weight with my hands flat on the floor.

"Look at me."

Again no resistance. As his eyes met mine, I pushed into the heat of his body. All I wanted was to slam home and make him mine, but I had no idea if he'd done this before.

"Have you been fucked before?" I growled, kicking myself for not checking.

"Yes."

He groaned and tried to push onto me, but I held back. I wouldn't hurt him.

"Dav, I'm good. I promise. Now get your dick inside me," he demanded, frustration clear in his voice.

I let that demand slide, but only because it was exactly what I wanted, too. I watched his face, but the sight of him with his head thrown back in ecstasy was too much. Fucking hell, he was breathtaking. I groaned and captured his lips with mine, kissing him, claiming him as I inched in, pushing against the tightness of his body. He whimpered and groaned, bearing down until the internal muscle of his body relaxed and I sank into his heat. The deeper I got, the more frantic our lips and bodies became until I was grinding against his balls.

"More..." Elliot groaned, his hands fisted before he gave up trying to hold them above his head and grabbed my hips, curling his fingers into my flesh, his almost black gaze holding mine.

I grunted at the pleasurable sting of his nails scoring my skin and pulled back before thrusting inside.

"Oh, gods...so...good," I rasped, moving harder and faster.

Lost in the feel of him and the way his hands gripped me, urging me on, I increased my pace, hammering into his tight body, our moans and pants mixing. My balls tightened, and I knew I was close. Changing my angle, I slammed into him hard. He yelled my name, his voice thick with pleasure, and I'd never heard anything so fucking hot.

"You feel so good," I growled in his ear, his whimpers and pleas urging me on. "I want to watch you fall apart." My fangs ached, I wanted to take his blood, to seal our bond, but no matter how good he felt, I wouldn't do that. I couldn't. He wasn't really mine, no matter what I said. He might never be. Fear and anger at my helplessness mixed with my lust, driving me harder.

"Oh gods, Dav, I'm so close..."

"Good, then scream my name when you come," I commanded, driving against his prostate until he yelled, my name falling from his lips as warmth spurted against my belly. The feel of him squeezing down on my cock was too much. My orgasm exploded through me, stealing my breath until I saw stars. I rode it out, my pleasure ebbing slowly, leaving my body sated and shuddering. Sucking in some deep breaths, mini spasms of pleasure gripped me as I came down from the most intense pleasure high I'd ever experienced. Carefully I released Elliot's legs and collapsed forward, catching myself so as not to crush him. I balanced on my elbows, reaching up to touch his flushed cheeks. My stomach tightened, a deep coldness settling in my chest, right behind that pull I felt towards him.

Slowly I pulled out of his body. I wanted to get up and leave, to run from what I'd just done, but his wince got to me.

"Are you okay? Did I hurt you?"

"No." His eyes sought out mine, a post-orgasmic haze in their depths. He was everything I'd thought he would be and more, but I made myself look away, hardening my heart. He was right; I *was* a damned liar just as he said.

Elliot tensed, his hand cupping my jaw as I went to move. "Dav? Please. Don't pull away from me," he whispered, his voice breaking.

I ground my molars, my teeth creaking. This was for the best. If I got any closer or couldn't resist the call of his blood, it would deepen our bond, and ultimately I wasn't powerful enough to end Count Balthazar Rossi. No vampire was. If Balthazar passed a death judgement, there was only one thing I could do to save Elliot's life. Beg. And if Balthazar honoured my request to let him live, then I would have to let Elliot go.

I swallowed down the lump in my throat as I leaned over and grabbed my t-shirt, my heart heavy. If my mate wanted to leave, I'd let him, no matter if it would rip my heart out. And the only way I could let Elliot go was to keep from bonding with him.

Being with me had to always be a choice.

9

Elliot

Birds twittered outside the shuttered bedroom window. Sighing, I reached over and clicked on the bedside light. Sleep had eluded me, not only in the last five hours, but for days. It had nothing to do with my room or the bed I was currently lying on. The damn place was the most luxurious bedroom I'd ever been in. The bed was huge and soft and covered in dark red silk bedding. There was a thick carpet that my toes sank into, and pretty paintings of the ocean and the castle hung on the walls. It was spotlessly clean and warm...and I hated it. No matter the expensive furnishing, or the wardrobe full of new clothes, it was empty—like my chest had felt since Davlov had basically thrown me out of his room.

He hadn't listened to my plea and had withdrawn from me completely. Oh, he was still polite, always making sure I was well fed and had everything I needed, but he was as distant emotionally as he could get. Tears pricked my eyes. It hurt more than any beating or injury I'd ever endured. I'd never felt pleasure, or a connection like I had a week ago in that gym. Desire spread right through me, those memories making me hard, just like they had done every day and night since.

I groaned, pulling a pillow over my face. It clearly hadn't been as good for an ancient and experienced vampire like Dav, despite his groans and whispers to the contrary. He'd withdrawn from the dirty half-blood quicker than any lover I'd ever had. Oh, he'd cleaned me up after our encounter, he'd even walked me to this room, but he'd already left me and we both knew it.

I tried to ignore the pain of his rejection and lies, but it stung to know he was just like every other vampire I'd ever known. I guessed even for Originals, a half-blood wasn't worth anything. I threw the covers off and sat on the side of the bed. At least a human's blood was pure enough to drink. According to Davlov, other supernatural blood was forbidden to Originals unless you wished to mark them as yours. I scoffed. Victor had never been bothered by that kind of rule. Mades drank supernatural blood to make themselves stronger; to give them the same strength and speed as an Original, even if it was only a temporary fix.

Dav hadn't even tried to take my blood while he fucked me. He really had no interest in me belonging to him, even though he'd told me I was his. Then again, he'd said he wouldn't let me leave his side, and look at where I ended up; sleeping alone in a bedroom far from his. I guess all his words were lies.

Curling my top lip, I pushed away the ache in my chest and glanced at the clock. Seven PM. Time for my lesson. Why Dav still insisted on me training, I had no idea. He just said I needed to have better skills if I was to take my revenge when I went home. We both knew I might not survive past the Count's return, but even if by some miracle I did, those words were just another slap in the face. It was clear that he wanted me gone.

My heart raced at the thought of the Count's return, but as always there was nothing I could do. I rubbed my chest where it ached emptily. The compulsion kept me from running, and I sure as shit couldn't hope to fight off a vampire as powerful as the

Count. I shook my head. Maybe he'd order Dav to kill me. My stomach rolled at the thought that Dav would do it, too.

Since my captor had made it clear he wasn't interested, I'd done everything he asked. There seemed little point in defying him. Besides, he only ever spoke to me to correct my posture, readjust my technique with a weapon, or demand I hit harder and faster. Out of the training gym, he barked at me to eat and sleep more. And that was it.

Vito had watched us with a stupid smirk on his face. Every chance he got, he'd tried goading me into losing my temper, or tempting me to defy Dav. Why, I didn't know. But the deliberate looks he gave Dav when he spoke to me made me think he was trying to piss off his boss as much as torment me. Yesterday he'd gotten his wish. Exhausted, hungry, and simmering with resentment for my situation, I'd lost my shit the moment Vito had drawled about my human side making me weak and not good enough to train with, or fuck, a vampire like Davlov Zoltar.

Dav had just watched with hard eyes and a dark expression as Vito had kicked my arse—until I was on the ground and every instinct in me came alive. Anger had flooded my veins, making me see red. I was furious at the lies Dav had told, at the Count for his compulsion, at Victor for being a lying and abusive bastard, at my mother for getting pregnant with me in the first place, but most of all at myself for never being strong enough to change my own godsdamned life.

Adrenaline and strength had shot into my muscles. It had shocked the shit out of me to feel pain in my gums and discover a set of sharp fangs protruding from under my upper lip. I'd concentrated on my surging anger instead of the hunger that raged through me, caught Vito's boot as he'd walked away, and flipped him to the ground. Without pause, I'd jumped across his hips and pummelled my fists into his face until he was a laughing and groaning, bloodied mess.

Dav had pulled me off. "Leave," was all he'd said, the snarl in his voice letting me know how close to the surface his vampire side was. Of course, I'd done exactly what he said, not just because of the compulsion, but because I was suddenly done being *nothing*. I'd promised myself then and there I would change my fate.

That was yesterday. Today I'd have to face his anger for hurting one of his men.

It might as well be now. I washed and shaved, then dressed in a clean pair of combats, I pulled on some socks and boots and grabbed a t-shirt. I'd eaten a whole large pizza and salad this morning before bed, but my stomach rumbled painfully. I rubbed it, sick of being so godsdamned hungry all the time. I straightened, annoyed when my trousers fell to my hips. Jesus, I was losing weight, too, not gaining it. It was ridiculous. How much did a vampire need to eat? Was I ill? Perhaps I should talk to Dav about a doctor. I laughed, the bitter sound echoing around the perfect room, making it sound even more empty.

"What's the fucking point in that, you idiot? You could be dead any day now. And if you're not, you're leaving." I pulled open the door and headed downstairs.

Voices drifted up from the kitchen. My heart sank. Vito...and Davlov.

Was this where the beating came? Punishment for yesterday? I'd never lost my temper like that before. I'd certainly never been strong enough to cause damage to someone. Then again, I'd never discovered my vampire side before. I flexed my fists and halted. For the first time in my life I'd felt strong, but smashing up Vito's face hadn't made me feel good. No, I'd felt guilty, spending most of the night worrying that I'd hurt him and made yet another enemy. Not only that, I hated that Dav had been furious with me for my loss of control. Vito had been trying to elicit that kind of reaction all week, and I'd disappointed Dav by letting him get to me.

A dull *thud...thud...thud...*drummed in my ears. I shook my head, almost cutting my tongue on my new fangs. They weren't large, but they were damned sharp. Despite living with them, I had very little idea about being a vampire, but I'd deal with it. Right now, I was starving. I needed food, and that meant facing the music. Taking a breath I stepped into the kitchen, unsurprised when the conversation stopped. I cleared my throat as two powerful gazes swung my way, the weight of them making me want to run.

"Uhh, hi." I attempted a smile, nerves fizzing in my belly.

Thud...

Thud...

Thud...

I shook my head again, trying to rid myself of that incessant noise, my attention snapping to Dav. My heart stuttered. Dav crossed his arms over his chest and glared at me, before shifting his attention to Vito. I had to force my gaze from the dark expression on his gorgeous face to look at Vito. My eyes widened. The cocky vamp was unblemished, no evidence of my uncontrolled rage visible.

Vito coughed, his gaze bouncing between us. If anything, he looked remorseful, not angry.

I wanted to back away when he walked towards me, but I'd already made the decision never to back down again. I'd discovered the strength and fury of my vampire side, and though it was buried deep, I'd managed to free it yesterday. I'd manage it again if I needed to.

Vito had spent the week giving me shit whenever he could. He'd goaded me, but I sensed he'd been trying to make me, or perhaps even Dav, lose control. He'd also worked with me, trained with me, and helped me. Because of that, I hadn't let my control slip until he told me I wasn't good enough for Dav. I'd believed he was right, but that was before I'd proved I could be as much vampire as I was human.

It was time to prove it again.

They were both skillful warriors and deserved my respect, not my uncontrolled anger.

My stomach cramped as that damned thudding stole my

focus. I shook it off once more and opened my mouth to apologise to them both.

"I owe you an apology," Vito interjected before I could speak, holding out his hand.

My mouth snapped shut. He was apologising to me?

He grinned sheepishly. "I was fucking with you yesterday. Mainly to wind up my boss. He's never been so fucked up over anyone as he is you, so even though you kicked my arse, I'm not sorry I did it. He needed to admit what you are to him, and how fucking amazing you are for all you have endured." His huge shoulders rose and fell in a shrug, a roguish smile curling his lips. "Besides, you needed to realise the same thing, and the only way to get you to do that was by releasing your vampire nature. It's been locked away for too long."

Too stunned to respond, I just took his hand. He slapped my shoulder with his other hand. "Don't worry, he kicked my arse harder than ever when you'd gone...you know? For upsetting you, hurting you, and generally being a dick."

"I—um, right," I managed to murmur, my attention flicking to Dav. He studied me steadily, his face tight. My mouth watered at the sight of his muscled arms crossed over his chest. My gaze travelled lower of its own accord across his flat stomach to the front of his combats, hiding what I knew was an impressive package... I swallowed hard. One I wanted. Right. Fucking. Now.

A low growl came from his chest, his eyes holding mine when my gaze snapped up to his face.

Thud...

Thud...

Thud...

Gods, I was *hungry.*

I inhaled Davlov's seductive scent, a growl resonating from my own chest.

"Okaaay," murmured Vito, releasing my hand. "I'll get back to work and leave you two alone..." He slapped my shoulder once more. "I'll be honoured to teach and train with you anytime, Elliot."

"Thanks," I managed to murmur. "I will—if I'm not dead."

His brows drew down, and he glanced at Dav clearly expecting his boss to dispute I was going to die.

Silence.

"Right," Vito murmured. "I'll see you soon, kid." And he left.

More silence, thick and charged with tension.

Dav grabbed a plate of bacon from the microwave and plonked it on the table with some fresh bread rolls and butter. He grabbed a mug and filled it with coffee, before slamming that down, too.

"Eat," he growled.

Something inside me snapped. "Fuck off. You eat."

His gaze rose to my face, dark and dangerous. "What?" His quiet question sent goosebumps racing over my skin.

I stretched my neck. There was nothing. No pain at my defiance, only that ever growing tug towards him, mixed with that *thud, thud, thud...* It was louder the closer he got to me. I cocked my head and swallowed hard. His heartbeat! I could hear his fucking heart beating, even sense the blood surging under his skin. Need raced through me at the tension in his powerful body. My gums ached and my whole being screamed with hunger.

"You heard me," I growled, stalking towards him, drawn to the quickening drum of his heart, and the rush of blood in his veins. He watched me, rising to my challenge, just like I knew he would.

Fuck! I wanted him.

Craved him.

Instinctively, I snarled and rubbed my tongue along my canines.

He straightened his spine, a muscle ticking in his jaw. "Eat your fucking breakfast, Elliot."

That growling, overbearing tone just pissed me off more. My fangs lengthened and I snarled, giving him a full view of them.

His whole body locked up, a dangerous light reflecting in his eyes. Driven by instinct and such lust I could barely think straight, I rushed forward and smacked the flat of my hand on his hard chest. Grabbing his shirt, I slammed him into the marble worktop.

"I am," I growled. "You."

His eyes widened a second before I moved, sinking my new teeth into the soft skin of his neck. I had no idea what I was doing, but I didn't need to; my body knew.

Big hands grabbed me, but not to push me away. I was pulled closer, one hand twisting in my hair and another clawing at my back. Blood hit the inside of my mouth and that was it, I was lost. I'd never tasted anything so delicious. My lips latched on to his hot skin and I sucked—hard. Warmth flooded my mouth at the same time as it flooded my limbs. My cock punched against my zipper, aching, painful, and ready. I slammed my hips forward rubbing desperately against Davlov's rigid length.

"Oh fuck,El." His groan only fired me up more. I'd never felt so turned on in my whole life, so hungry for anyone. I released my hold on his shirt, dropped my hand to the button of his combats, flicked it open and fumbled with the zipper. I half expected him to push me away or stop me, but he didn't. His hard panting breaths and loud moans were like a drug. I sucked harder just as I wrapped a hand around his steel length.

"Elliot...shit..." His words turned into a deep, pleasured rumble as I worked him with my fist. "Fuck it..." he muttered and I felt him fumble with my own button and zipper before he pulled me out. "Move," he ordered, shoving my hand away. I snarled, but did as he said, unwilling to release his neck from my hold. I doubted I could even if I wanted to. My instincts had taken over. I needed his blood like I needed air to breathe. Strength like nothing I'd felt before seeped deep into my bones. It was my turn to groan when he mashed my cock up against his and grabbed us both in his calloused hand, working us in tandem.

My jaw went lax, pleasure from his touch making my knees weak.

"Don't you dare fucking stop. Suck. Feed on me, baby. Take what you need."

I latched back on with my lips and did exactly what he said, swallowing over and over as he pumped his fist up and down.

This wasn't just sex. It was something else. It was hard and raw and earth-shattering. That pull on my chest grew almost painful, but I paid it no mind, too lost in Dav's taste and touch.

My orgasm built quickly. I tried to let go, to tell him, but I couldn't bear the thought of releasing his neck.

"Elliot...dammit. I-I can't...hold on..."

A deep low growl rolled up my throat as I took a strong hard draw of his spicy blood. He exploded, bellowing his pleasure, warmth spilling over our skin and his fingers. My own climax rocketed through me, every cell in my body on fire, my muscles locked tight. I couldn't contain my roar, unlatching my teeth to let it free. Spasms shuddered through me for so long I thought I'd pass out. I gripped on for dear life to the solid wall of muscle that was Davlov, dropping my head to his shoulder, panting and utterly spent as I slowly came down. I trembled, wrapping my arms around him not wanting to leave the warmth of his body.

I stayed like that until my breathing started to calm, but pain yanked at my heart when I realised how still he was. I pulled back, but my attention snapped to the blood leaking from the two puncture wounds in his neck. Puncture wounds I'd made. The sight made me feel satisfied and a whole heap of other emotions I couldn't begin to name. His blood ran down the strong column of his neck in twin rivulets, soaking his skin and tee. I inhaled, licked my lips and growled. "*Mine.*"

His throat bobbed. "If you lick the wounds they will heal," he said, his voice hoarse.

My nostrils flared. I didn't want to heal them. I wanted everyone to know what I'd done. But I hated how still he was. How quiet. Slowly, I leaned in and dragged my tongue over the wounds. Dav's breath caught when I hummed. "Damn you are the best thing I've ever tasted," I told him truthfully.

His cock twitched against mine, but he let us both go. "Was that your first taste of blood?"

I blinked, my heart stuttering at the empty tone in his voice. "Yes."

I frowned, I'd never even considered taking blood before, but I'd known exactly what to do with him. I also knew I'd never want anyone else's. Only his.

"Then that's why." He pushed me back a few steps, steadying me when I stumbled. "You should go and rest before it hits you."

Now I was really confused, by his words and yet another withdrawal. What I'd felt had been mind blowing in every way. Clearly, it meant absolutely nothing to him.

"Before what hits me? The after effects of the blood? *Your* blood? Or the fact that you're backing the fuck away from me again like I'm some pariah!"

Dav grabbed a towel and threw it at me. "Clean yourself up." He tucked himself away without bothering to wipe our cooling cum off his skin, then turned his back on me. "Go and rest, Elliot. You're going into bloodlust."

"Bloodlust?"

Bloodlust was for full blooded vamps hitting maturity, or newly fledged vampires to finish their transition into a Made. Victor had told me half-bloods didn't transition. My hands shook. But Victor had lied to me about just about everything.

"Yes. Fuck, Elliot! Just listen to me! Go! Go and lock yourself in your godsdamned room right now!" he bellowed. "I have to leave!"

I swallowed. "You're going? After what we just shared?"

"I have a damned job to do. One that doesn't include helping you discover your vampire nature. It's too dangerous for us both. I'll get some blood sent up to you. Drink it as soon as it arrives, it will dull the cravings. If you're lucky your human side will prevent the need for sex."

Ice crept into my heart, pushing away the hope and...love... that had bloomed in my chest for this moody, insufferable, yet utterly bewitching vampire. He was so damned bossy—and caring—when he let himself be. But right then, he was being an total bastard. Gods, he'd looked after me from the moment he'd taken me prisoner. He'd made me eat, given me the skills to take my revenge, made me feel stronger, like I could actually be somebody—until he'd ripped that hope away. I shook my head. I was so stupid. No matter the physical draw between us, he didn't need a half-blood, he needed his freedom; he was too ancient, too powerful, too *everything*, to be tied to me. The scent of me on him would fade quickly. I wasn't *vampire* enough for it to linger, nor was this ever likely to happen again. That was as clear as fucking crystal. My eyes burned, but I forced my chin up.

"Yeah? Don't worry, if it doesn't, I won't bother you, I'll visit Vito or one of the others, they can help me through it."

"No they fucking can't," he snarled. "You're off limits. None of them will touch you."

"None of them will touch the dirty half-breed, is that it? Especially not you! Fuck you, Dav."

I walked away from him, leaving him to storm in the opposite direction right out through the back door. He was right, I felt drunk. The corridors tilted, the metallic and addictive taste of his blood still on my tongue when I stumbled and fell to my knees. Tears rolled down my cheeks.

"I hate you," I whispered.

It felt like hours before I could summon enough energy to get to my feet. Exhausted, I staggered into my room, locked the door and fell face first onto the bed, passing out.

avlov

I opened the SUV's door for Sorcha and helped her down.

"Thank you, Davlov." Her sweet voice and shy smile eased the tension in my body. I took a steadying breath and nodded. The blonde-haired, alluring human looked at the Count.

He nodded to her, giving her a small smile. "Go on in, Sorcha. Go and rest. I need to talk to Dav. I also have some work to do tonight, so I will see you tomorrow."

"Okay." She glanced up at me before quickly dropping her gaze to the ground. "See you later, Dav."

I nodded at her though she didn't see.

Bal waited until she'd gone inside. "How is Elliot?"

His question had me snapping to attention, and I couldn't stop a low growl resonating from me. My heart thundered as he raised a brow. I ran a hand through my hair. For once it was unkempt. I'd not even shaved that morning. But the thought of my Lord hurting Elliot was killing me. I was ready to destroy this whole fucking estate, even lose my life if it meant Elliot would stand a chance of getting away.

The Count prowled towards me. He was taller than my six feet four, and though he was solidly muscled, he was sleek and looked like he'd just stepped from the pages of GQ magazine. He was lethal. His black hair hung down his back in a long braid, his pale, almost colourless eyes not missing a thing. He studied me intently, and I tensed when I felt his firm grip on my fisted hands.

"Breathe, Dav." His eyes narrowed. "So, he is definitely your mate." It was more a statement than a question.

I swallowed hard. There was no point in denying it. "Yes."

He angled his head slightly. "And you would fight me to save him?"

I blinked, a battle raging in my soul. I both loved and hated that I would. I was devoted to my Lord and friend, and would never betray him, but Elliot was mine. My mate, and the only one I would ever give up everything for—including my life.

A small smile pulled on the corners of the Count's mouth. "Your silence tells me all I need to know, my friend."

My heart lurched.

The Count peered up at the castle windows. "Where is he?"

"No, I won't tell you..." I croaked, wishing I'd gotten Elliot out. But he was in bloodlust. There was no way he could survive on the run while he transitioned. Selfishly, I'd wanted him where I could make sure he had everything he needed.

Except you... a little voice added.

Now Bal was going to kill him...

My whole body tensed, my vampire side punching forward. I roared. "You will not hurt him!" I yanked my fists from the Count's grasp and punched out at his stomach, hitting air. He'd moved sideways faster than I could see.

"Elliot! Run!" I bellowed, hoping he'd hear me from the open window of his room. I hadn't been the one to take him the bags of blood he needed to survive, but Vito told me he was doing okay, putting on weight and being a grumpy bastard, but okay.

Like the sad idiot I was, I'd asked if he'd mentioned me. Vito had laughed until he cried, and told me to stop being a prick, get up there and talk to Elliot myself.

I spun, hating myself for not getting Elliot away sooner, but the Count hadn't told me he was on his way back. He'd landed at the private airfield, and by the time I'd gotten there, he'd been waiting for me. I'd had no time.

"Davlov! Stop this, right now!" roared the Count from behind me.

I ignored him and ran as fast as I could up to Elliot's room. The Count caught me, slamming me against the wall outside Elliot's room. His fist connected with my jaw, knocking me down.

"Dav! Enough!" he snapped, a powerful wave of compulsion accompanying his words. I was too damned old for it to hold me for long, but it was enough to still me even though every instinct I had urged me to protect my mate.

"Balthazar, please, don't hurt him." I'd do it. I'd beg for his life...

The Count's elegant features twisted, and I swore he looked affronted.

"Hurt him? I'll pretend you didn't just insult our centuries old friendship. I'd never hurt him, not when he's your mate. What do you take me for?" He leaned down and held out his hand. "Now get up off the floor and introduce me to the man who has stolen your ice-cold heart."

For a moment my brain didn't compute his words. "W-what?"

He sighed and straightened his suit, dropping his hand. "I was never going to hurt him, Dav. He wasn't ever a real threat. If he was, I'd have ended him that night. Do you really think you were the only one to watch a half-blood stranger wandering around my club? One who was totally unknown to me and in my territory? One who had no interest in the other entertainments the club had to offer? He had no clue how to behave, or what to do there. He didn't go anywhere except to the bar, and then spent each night watching me. He has scars all over his hands and he moved like a killer, except there was no murderous light in his eyes. He was a paradox. One that intrigued me, especially when you became fixated on him."

I climbed off the floor, feeling both foolish and so relieved my hands trembled. "I assumed you were too busy to notice him."

There was the tiniest hint of a smile. "Oh, I was, but when my second's attention was stolen by a mortal, I paid attention. Plus, I smelt the garlic on him as soon as he moved close to me. It's disgusting stuff. It wasn't hard to figure out he was going to try and kill me."

I dusted myself off, still trying to comprehend Bal's reasoning. "Why did you bother to compel him, or threaten his life if you had no intention of punishing him?" I blew out a heavy breath and shook my head. Why did I think, even for a moment, that Bal would harm my mate? Embarrassment heated my face.

"Dav, don't beat yourself up over this. You are doing what any vampire who has found his mate would do. You're protecting him from every threat, including me."

"But I didn't. Shit! I've ignored him. I've left him alone to go through bloodlust for the past forty eight hours. I pulled away because I thought he was still under your compulsion to do as I said; to stay here. I wanted him to be safe, and I wanted him to stay, but only if he chose it. He's been lied to his whole life, he has no idea about a mate bond. He needs to know what it means before he makes a choice." I ran a hand through my hair, mussing it even more, and looked at him sheepishly. "I didn't want a bond to hold him here. I was prepared to beg you not to hurt him, and failing that, to tell him to run while I fought you."

"Wait," Bal held up a hand, and shook his head. "In all the hundreds of years of our friendship, that is the most confused reasoning I have ever heard from you."

I rubbed my face. "You're right. I am so fucked up over him. But if he stays, it has to be of his own free will, not because you compelled him to stay."

The Count chuckled. "Dav, that small amount of compulsion I used would only have lasted a few days, a week at the most. He's been here the rest of the time without any coercion from me. I wanted to give you time with him, to get to know him, and for him to know you. That's all my compulsion was for. I assumed by this point that you would have claimed him and him you." He glanced at the door. "Is that not the case?"

I swallowed hard, my heart beginning to race. "No, no it isn't because I fucked up. I pushed him away. I hurt him, and now he thinks he isn't good enough for me."

"Ah, I see. Well, I think it's time I meet Elliot properly. Then you can explain to him that he has his freedom. I'm sure once he knows he can leave, he won't. From what you've told me about Elliot's life, Victor Hamilton's coven is not somewhere he'll want to return."

"Maybe," I muttered, thinking about the vengeance Elliot wanted. Would he forgive me for leaving him alone to get through bloodlust? Jesus, I'd been a class A dick. He hadn't a clue about bloodlust or what to expect, and I'd abandoned him, leaving him to suffer through it alone. I raised my hand to knock on the door, then hesitated. I didn't deserve him after what I'd done.

"Dav?"

I took a breath, nodded at my friend and knocked gently. "Elliot? It's me, and the Count. It's safe, you can open the door. You will not be harmed. I promise."

Silence. My heart rate notched up, worry tightening my chest. I banged hard with my fist on the door. "Elliot? Open the damned door! Now! Or I'll break it down."

The Count caught my hand and smirked. "Probably not the best way to introduce him to me, my friend."

I actually flushed. "Sorry, I lose my commonsense where he's concerned."

"So I'm beginning to understand. Let's hope it settles a bit when you are mated."

I swallowed hard. "If he wants me after what I've done," I murmured.

The Count shrugged. "If he doesn't, persuade him. By any means necessary."

Before I could answer, he knocked politely on the door. "Elliot, this is Count Rossi. I give you my word that I have no intention of harming you, now or in the future. But I would like to meet you."

SIlence.

My anxiety spiked. Elliot would never hide. Something was wrong.

"That's it." I kicked the door open, bursting the lock.

The room was empty. Elliot's scent—and the coppery smell of blood—lingered in the air, but it was faint, as though he'd not been here recently. Panic slammed through me.

"No. No. No. No," I muttered as I rushed into the bathroom. It was empty. I spun back into the room. A shirt laid over the back of a chair. I snatched it up, gripping it in my fist as I threw open the wardrobe door. Most of his clothes were still there, but his combats, boots and jacket were gone. I slammed the door shut making the heavy structure rattle. Quelling my panic, I tried to think. Vito had seen Elliot yesterday when he'd brought the blood up, but no one else would have been near him.

Because you're a cruel and selfish son-of-a-bitch who abandoned your mate when he needed you most.

What the fuck had I done? I'd driven him away and killed any hope of him accepting me, that's what. And the worst of it was, I couldn't blame him, not even a little.

"Ahh!" I yelled, smashing my fist into the bedroom wall, leaving cracked plaster behind. "He's gone."

"Dav, he's a vampire in bloodlust he can't have gone far. He needs blood."

I shook my head. Elliot was clever and resourceful. He'd left as soon as the blood had been dropped off by Vito. That blood was enough to last through his cravings for twenty four hours at least. And I'd sent more than any starved vampire could ever need. It was my blood. I'd bled for him, leaving myself weak. It had been the only way to ease my guilt at leaving him alone. "No, he's gone. He left yesterday."

The Count frowned. "How do you know that?"

I met his steady gaze. "Because he's clever enough to have noticed when our deliveries arrive. He's used one of them to get off the estate. Vito and the others would never let him leave alone. They wouldn't have searched the vans leaving the estate, especially not for Elliot. Not when they know he's in lust."

"Fine. Then we hunt him down. He can't have got far."

I swallowed the ache in my throat and slumped against the wall. Desperation and self-loathing rose inside me. What kind of cold-hearted bastard left his mate alone to suffer through the desperate need for blood and the even more desperate need to fuck? Me...that's who. I panted, my breathing as ragged as it had been when he'd taken my blood and driven me to the edge of my control. I ground my teeth, my jaw muscles in spasm. The memory of the way he'd held me afterwards, like I was his whole world, like I was his everything, undid me. I released a roar of rage and pain, hitting the mirror with my fist, sending shards of glass flying across the room before I sank to my knees. No matter my reasons, I'd royally fucked up. I'd lost him...and destroyed myself in the process. There was no going back. No undoing what I'd done...

"Davlov! Get your damned arse up. We're going out to look for him, right now."

I slowly lifted my head, I wanted to so badly, but Elliot had chosen his path—he'd run. "No, Bal. Not this time. He chose to leave." Bitterness sat like a heavy stone in my stomach. "And I don't blame him, not one bit. I don't deserve him."

"You're just going to let him go?" Bal's words were careful, neutral.

Self-disgust and pain ripped through me. I growled. "Yes! Now back the fuck off, Count!"

Standing up, I met his gaze and held it. For a moment he allowed it, the weight of his power pushing on me. I didn't care that I'd just challenged him, that he could kick my arse from here to the underworld and back without breaking a sweat. I deserved it. I wanted it. I wanted to forget what I'd done...that Elliot was gone because I'd let him down. My fists curled and my fangs lengthened. I was spoiling for a fight...

But Bal just nodded and stepped over the shards of mirror, pulling open the broken door. "As you wish. Let me know when you come to your damned senses. I'll give you everything you need to find him."

Agony sliced me from the inside as I stood alone in that room. I lifted Elliot's shirt to my nose and inhaled, terror claiming me like I'd never known before. My mate was alone. He'd need more blood... He'd never want anyone else's blood, that's what he'd said, but he only had twenty four hours of my blood left at the most. He'd give in when the cravings took him; he'd have to or die. I roared into his shirt. My scent would fade from him, just as his would from me. I couldn't let that happen. Panting, I breathed in and out through the material of his shirt. Gods, what would my life be like without him? The thought of never being surrounded by his scent again, of never feeling his touch or touching him, shattered something in my heart. I gasped as pain hit me, and the tug behind my ribs exploded. I sank to my knees and fell forward, catching myself on the floor with my hands, Elliot's shirt still clutched in one of them. I'd be nothing but an empty shell without him...cold and hollow.

Jumping to my feet, I ran out of the door, my heart racing.

 lliot

Traffic rumbled along the road outside the Gambit.

Breathe... I told myself. But it was hard when I knew who was in there. I'd arrived here only a few minutes ago, and my skin itched with the need to storm in and make Davlov see me for more than some half-blood, too naive to know what I wanted— which was him. I wanted him more now than I ever had. My chest ached with emptiness, and I felt raw. I had since I'd punctured his skin, sucking the warm blood from his body, and he'd ripped my heart out by rejecting me.

I rubbed my face. Shit, was it really only forty eight hours since I'd walked away from him? It was pathetic to go back to someone who didn't want me; I knew that. But I couldn't stand the thought of never seeing him again.

I'd fought the lure of the blood Davlov had sent me until stomach cramps had made me scream. Hating that he'd force me to take some unknown person's blood, I'd sobbed and cursed his existence—until I'd discovered it was his. Swallowing that blood hadn't been the same as drinking from him, but it had calmed the hunger cramps to a level where I could cope. What it hadn't done was sate the lust in my body. The only thing that helped with that constant burn of need was to throw myself back into the memory of Dav and me together, using my fist until I was swollen and sore—and ready to hunt Davlov down and demand he help me, until I realised he hadn't been back to the castle since that night.

When I attacked Vito and demanded to know where he was, Vito had calmly told me Dav was staying elsewhere, and would find me when he was ready.

"You aren't a prisoner in your room, Elliot, but I can smell your need, your lust. Some of the other guards aren't strong enough to resist that call and will take what you will not freely give. Don't put them—or Dav—in that position. He will kill them if they force their blood, or other things, on you. Bloodlust is the one thing that will cause vampires to return to their base instincts."

"What base instincts?" I'd asked.

"Feeding and fucking, my friend," he'd said before leaving me to stew on those words.

"Only some of them," I'd muttered in disgust. It was obvious Davlov could easily resist me, even after claiming that I was his.

That knowledge had been a bitter pill to swallow. Revenge had seemed a better idea than sitting around waiting for either another painful rejection or death. I'd hidden myself in the laundry van that serviced the staff's living quarters. From my window I'd watched it arrive every Thursday morning since I'd been at the castle. All the bedsheets and towels were externally laundered, all except the main castle's. Dressed in my black combats, boots, t-shirt, and jacket, with a baseball cap over my brown curls, I'd looked like any other guard.

The guards watching the castle changed at eight am, which was right when the laundry van arrived. They had a quick handover before the night guards marched away to the security hub, and the day guards set off to patrol the castle perimeter. I'd been waiting, and as soon as they'd gone, I'd marched towards the van, just another guard after his shift was done. Deliberately, I'd barged into the laundry guy. He'd dropped the bags he carried. Helpfully, I'd picked them up telling him I'd put them in the van as an apology, giving him a sexy grin, and making him blush. Flustered, he'd let me, and I'd told him to jump in the driver's seat before chucking the bags in the back and slamming the door. Except I left it unlatched, and after he'd given me a wave in the mirror, I'd leapt onto the open door, swung into the van and closed it, burying myself under the stink of dozens of other vampires.

I smiled. The guards hadn't scented me or the bloodlust raging through my system when they'd given the van a cursory check. After all, who'd want to smuggle themselves out of the castle? Certainly not someone who needed a constant supply of blood.

I released a breath; none of them had taken into account my human side. I wasn't as lost in my transition to vampire as they'd all expected. I chose to see that as a good thing. Even the thought of taking blood or having sex with anyone other than Dav made me feel ill. The last lot of blood bags he'd sent with Vito were in my hotel room—empty, and I was fucking hungry.

Right, so I needed to grow some brass balls and confront him. I hadn't seen the car go past, but that meant nothing. He could still be in there. My heart rate thrummed faster and faster as I straightened off the wall and strode confidently across the street. No one glanced at me strangely. I was bigger now, not some skinny half-assed human.

When I'd arrived in London, I'd downed one of the blood bags, almost climaxing at the taste of Dav easing down my throat. I'd hungered with every part of my soul for him. That's when I'd broken. I needed to see him again, to prove that I wanted to be with him, and beg him to give me a chance. I had no idea how to manage that without the Count finding me, but it was a risk I was willing to take.

My stomach lurched. Gods, I'd been an idiot to believe

anything Victor said. He'd sent me to kill the most powerful vampire in existence with a fucking garlic-spiked ring! For fuck's sake, it amounted to nothing more than a toy in their eyes. It had been laughable as an assassination attempt; one Victor would have shown his contempt for by beating me unconscious before killing me like he'd promised if he hadn't actually given me the damned thing, knowing it wouldn't work. I'd been an expendable way to send a message.

Maybe if I offered to serve the Count he would let me live, let me pay for my sin against him that way? The image of the bespelled dancers threatened to steal my resolve, but I pushed it away. I'd risk anything for the chance to see Dav again.

I unfastened my too tight jacket, aware the soft material of my t-shirt moulded to my very recently developed muscles. As soon as I'd woken up from my blood haze, it had been obvious I was physically different. My muscles had grown, making my clothes tighter. My hair was longer and richer, my skin healthier, and my eyes had a darkness to them that was definitely vampire. I smirked, wondering what Dav would think of my new look, and prayed he'd find it hot.

"Shit," I muttered under my breath at the thought of facing him again. This whole idea could backfire, leaving me utterly broken if it turned out he didn't want me. But all the things he'd done to care for me and ensure my comfort convinced me he at least felt something. I lifted my chin. I hadn't lied when I'd told him he was mine. The ache behind my ribs had only increased, that knowledge undeniable after I'd swallowed his blood. He had taken root in my heart and soul, and nothing could change that. I'd been an idiot. I'd left Dav to try and protect a heart that was already his. Even vengeance was no longer important.

I nodded at the guards, who returned my greeting. They inhaled as I got close, their eyes widening. Neither of them stopped me. I smiled, knowing some of Dav's scent still lingered on me. Descending the stairs, my apprehension spiked. I hoped other vamps wouldn't smell my bloodlust, not after I'd just feasted on Dav's blood. Fighting off horny vampires was not my goal tonight or any night.

The guards at the bottom door hesitated for a moment before one pressed his earpiece, listening to the command being issued.

"Go on through," he motioned to the door, keeping his distance from me.

I swallowed and headed in. My unease grew as the handsy demon in the weapons search area just ushered me by instead of frisking me or offering to take my coat as she had before.

The club wasn't completely empty, but it wasn't packed either. Then again, it was early, only eleven PM on a Friday night. I didn't have any money, but I wasn't here to drink. I was here to make some noise and get noticed. Just not yet. I headed towards the empty fight ring and took a seat at a free table, which was hidden in the shadows. The Count's throne-like seat was empty. My heart sank, but I shook off my disappointment. It didn't mean anything. Dav could still be here.

To my right, three fae males sat at a table, casting openly interested glances my way. They were stunning to look at, and desire warmed my body, but they weren't my prey. I turned away, only to meet the gazes of three male and one female vampire who watched me, too. I smirked at them, holding each stare in turn. Small snarls curled their lips at my little challenge. My grin widened. How different I was to that scared boy who'd been in here only weeks ago. I glanced over at the back of the Gambit to where the sex club was hidden behind a purple curtain. I huffed a chuckle; why they bothered with that scrap of material, I didn't know. Not when the female vampire got on her knees and started sucking off one of the males in full view of everyone. Their eyes flicked my way.

Nothing. I felt absolutely nothing. Blood and sex may be what I needed, but not from them.

The room eventually filled, and I shucked off my jacket, revealing my more muscular torso through the t-shirt that clung to every contour of my chest, back and arms. I smiled. It felt good to know I looked hot for a change and not like I was half-starved. Because now I knew that's what Victor had done; he'd kept blood away from me and fed only my human side. It had been enough to keep me alive, but I'd never felt sated. I'd craved something, but hadn't known what. Not until Dav. Now he was all I wanted —or needed.

I continued to look around the room searching the shadows for any sign. Nothing. Music blared around me, glasses clinked, and voices bellowed, all vying to be heard in the din. I shuffled in my seat, getting impatient. The fae still watched. They did nothing for me, not even the tall, white-haired, beautiful male, who was eye fucking me like I was his next meal. Waves of dominance rolled off him, yet, for the first time in years, I didn't care. I didn't feel weak; I felt powerful. He wanted me... I glanced at the other fae, and the vampires. They all did.

My attention was snagged by Count Balthazar as he stalked to his chair, leading a bald headed, beautiful woman covered in runes by a collar and leash. Her eyes flashed with hatred and disdain as she surveyed the crowd before he ordered her to kneel at his feet. His eyes turned my way, and my heart lurched until I realised he was looking over my head towards the bar. I turned. The blonde-haired girl who'd served Dav and me smiled shyly at him.

If the Count was here, I hoped that meant Dav would be, too, or this was going to go very wrong.

I rolled my shoulders and closed my eyes. Focusing inwards, I pulled my vampire side closer to the surface. My gums stung as my fangs lengthened. Time to get this show on the road. I stood right in the Count's eyeline, blocking his view of the blonde. His snarl sent my blood cold, but I saw the moment he recognised me. We locked eyes, and he gave an almost imperceptible nod of his head.

My heart raced, and blood rushed through my veins as I waited. There was only one reason I would dare come here, and the Count knew it. At least he hadn't killed me on sight. That had to be good, didn't it? Seconds later, Dav materialised at the Count's side. My eyes widened. He'd told me older vampires could dematerialise and reappear where they willed, but I'd never seen it. He leaned down and listened to the Count's words before his head snapped towards me.

I swallowed. He was pale, had at least two days growth of stubble, and looked exhausted, yet he was still the most breathtaking sight I'd ever seen in my life. I gave him a tentative smile. His throat bobbed, and he mouthed, "Don't fucking move." Then he was gone.

A hand landed on my shoulder, and I let myself be turned, a relieved smile on my face until I saw both the fae and the vampires surrounding me. I registered the white-haired fae just as he grabbed my forearms, forcing them into my sides as he pressed his nose—and mouth—into my neck. Before I understood what was happening, big hands grabbed my t-shirt, pulled it from my waistband and slid up my back.

"Don't be shy, fledgling, tell me your name," purred a seductive voice.

"I-I, it's, um…" I blinked and shook my head. It felt like I had cotton wool in my brain. I couldn't think…until something sharp scraped my neck.

"No!" I roared. Pulling free, I reared back, headbutting the fae on the bridge of his nose. He grunted, blood gushing from his nostrils. No way was anyone claiming me or my blood. His friends moved quicker than I could and grabbed my arms, holding back the punch I aimed at his face.

He spat blood from his mouth. "Oh, sweetness, you're so mine," he drawled, blood staining his teeth. Fear punched through me. I was no match for six supernatural males.

Dav had to be here soon…

"Fuck you," I snarled.

"You will until you're begging for mercy."

In the blink of an eye, the fae's sinister grin disappeared, and he grunted, pain twisting his features before he flew backwards, hitting other patrons as he crashed through the crowd and slammed into the bar.

Davlov stood there looking like an avenging nightmare, his head dipped, looking up through heavy brows, his eyes burning with fury. He slowly moved his head and they gleamed red like the reflection of an animal in the dark. His hands were open, his nails sharp, lethal and dripping with blood. Fae blood. The vampires slowly backed off, their hands raised. This was the Count's lethal second in command, and they had more sense than to take him on. They turned and left. He snarled and eyed the fae who held me.

"Let my mate go, right fucking now, and I'll kill you quickly. Don't, and you'll suffer over and over." The air around him shook, small sparks of energy biting at my exposed skin. Gods, he was pissed—and totally magnificent.

Together the two fae pulled me backwards.

"Fuck. Fuck. Fuck." I heard one swear.

I smiled. "Yes, you are. Totally."

"He comes with us. Let us go, and he lives. Hunt us, and we'll enjoy him before he dies."

"You gonna stand for that, baby?" Dav snarled, his gaze locking with mine.

Gods damn, he was sexy with his fangs down and his vampire side unleashed.

My smile was just for him before I yanked my arms from my captors, spun and punched one square in the face, breaking his teeth before pivoting and kicking the other on the side of his head with my boot heel. They both staggered backwards.

Davlov moved.

A second later, he snapped their necks and flung their bodies aside. I looked away from that macabre sight. Instead, my gaze was pulled to Dav's face. My heart slammed against my ribs, the pull I always felt towards him tugging me forward. He stepped close to me, leaving only a few inches of space between us.

"Hi," I whispered, my mouth so dry I could barely speak.

A sexy smile curled his lips, and all I wanted was to claim them, but things were so uncertain between us I daren't move for fear of him rejecting me. His eyes softened to that beautiful hazel that I loved.

"Hi, yourself."

I started to speak, to tell him how sorry I was.

"Wait..." he said, and pulled something from the back pocket of his jeans. "Give me your hand, Elliot," he rumbled.

I did. Immediately.

He blinked slowly, releasing a shaky breath. Taking it in a gentle grip, he placed something in my palm. Warm metal dug in my skin as he curled my fingers closed around the item.

"I thought you'd be on a plane to Europe by now," he murmured.

I shook my head, so focused on him, nothing else existed. "Revenge doesn't matter to me, Dav." I lifted my other hand and cupped his face. "Only you do."

His shoulders rose and fell as he released another shaky breath and gave a small nod. "You came here to find me? You risked your freedom, your life, for me?"

I swallowed hard and glanced at the Count, who raised his glass to me. "Yes."

Dav held my chin and pulled my attention back towards him before leaning in. "Well, don't do it again."

I groaned at his closeness, gasping when his mouth brushed my jaw.

"But you can relax; you're safe here. No one will hurt you in this club ever again, El. Not now they know..." he murmured against my skin.

Blood rushed in my ears, hunger rearing up as his scent surrounded me. My legs trembled. "Know what?"

"That you are mine. That you always will be." His mouth slanted over mine in the most sensuous kiss I'd ever had. His tongue slid against mine, dominating me, tasting every part of my mouth. I was heedless of where we were or how many people watched. I didn't care. If this was him claiming me, then I was claiming him right back. I grabbed him, ready to fuck him right there on the floor. I didn't give a shit who saw, not when it meant every godsdamned supernatural and human in our world would know who I belonged to and who belonged to me. But Dav gently drew back, catching my lower lip between his teeth and dragging it with him as he pulled away. I winced, so he let go, a satisfied look in his eyes as he licked my blood off his fang. He tapped my fist, the one holding the piece of metal.

"Not here. If you still want me, if you can forgive me for being such a stupid bastard, then I'll meet you at home."

Confused, I looked down and opened my fist. An old style key etched in vampire runes sat in my palm. I swallowed hard. There was only one door that it would fit. I looked up to ask him why he'd given it to me, but he wasn't there. My heart lurched in panic, making me spin towards the Count, who smiled and gestured for me to go to him. Confused, I almost ran to the vampire lord, wondering if Dav had told him where he was going.

"Where is he? Where's he gone?" I almost shouted, anxiety getting the better of me. Apprehension burst through me when I realised I'd just yelled at Count Balthazar Rossi. He merely looked at me, his disturbing eyes gleaming. He lounged back in his chair, an elbow on the carved chair arm, his fingers and thumb grasping his chin, and one leg crossed over the other. He was the epitome of a composed and lethal vampire lord.

"Calm yourself, young one. He is waiting at the castle for you."

My heart sank. How the hell was I going to get back to the castle?

The Count gave a deep chuckle. "My car is already waiting outside to take you to the airfield. The helicopter will have you back home in just over an hour."

I nodded, trying not to collapse to my knees in relief. Desperate to get to Dav, I turned away.

"Elliot!" His commanding voice stopped me in my tracks.

"Yes," I managed to say. My pulse thundered, the tension in my shaking muscles almost unbearable. Dav's taste lingered on my tongue, and it was driving me mad not having him near me to touch, and kiss—to bite.

"You're about to hit your full bloodlust, I can sense it." He smiled. "Try not to drain my second dry. I need him around for another six hundred years."

"Six hundred years?" I breathed, my eyes wide.

"That's right. And in all that time I've never seen him fall for anyone. You are his mate, making you one of the only people alive who could hurt or break him." His eyes turned to ice. "If you do, I will hunt you down and end everything about you. Then I will bring you back from death and do it over and over again. Do I make myself clear?"

I nodded, unable to speak past the fear and respect I felt at that moment. The Count loved my man, and although that warning scared the shit out of me, it also warmed my heart. Dav was protected as fiercely as he protected the Count. "You do, Lord Rossi."

He grinned. "Oh, I think we can dispense with formality, certainly while no one else is around, don't you? You will belong to my friend, and he to you, that makes you family—my family. You can call me Count or Bal when we are in the confines of the castle. If we are in public, or you are working for me, Lord or Count will do."

"Yes, Count."

"Good. Now go. He's waiting for you."

"Thank you," I said quietly.

"Go." He made a grand dismissive gesture with his hand, but he smirked at me as he did. I turned and jumped off the stage before I broke into a run, heading through the club and sprinting up the stairs. I didn't give a shit at that moment that the most powerful vampire lord in existence had just given me his blessing to claim his second and basically invited me into his family. All I cared about was getting to Davlov.

lliot

My legs bounced impatiently. The helicopter landed, and before I was given the all clear to jump out, I threw off my headset and leapt, my feet slamming into the ground. Cold air buffeted me, and goosebumps rose on my skin. My reaction wasn't because of the cold, though. It was nervous excitement and raging desire. I was going to claim Dav tonight. I'd make him see sense and use everything in my power to make him admit we were stronger together.

The headlights of an SUV flickered at me. I jogged towards them, my heart pounding. Had Dav come to pick me up?

I threw the door open, ready to jump him right there.

"Oh, it's you."

"Hey, don't look so fucking disappointed, kid," Vito said, with a shit eating grin.

I rolled my eyes. "No offence, old man, but your ugly mug isn't the one I want to see."

He chuckled. "I get it. I really do."

"Yeah? Well, put your foot down then, I've got a mate to claim."

"Ain't that the truth? Maybe when you both sort your shit out, he won't threaten to rip our heads off every damned day."

"He did that?"

Vito just peered at me and raised his brows. "I've never seen him so messed up. He hated leaving you to go through bloodlust alone. Poor bastard had to force himself to stay away, even after he'd bled himself almost dry to give you enough blood to survive. He even threatened to rip my throat out if I didn't keep my hands off you when I delivered the stuff." He started the car. "And when he discovered you'd left...well, broken doesn't do justice to how he looked."

I rubbed my hand over my chest, my heart aching. "I didn't mean to hurt him like that. I thought he didn't want me."

"Yeah, well, you're both a pair of bloody pricks. He hurt you, you hurt him, and all that hearts and roses shit. Now you can both fix it, and the rest of us can breathe easy again." He pulled up at the back door of the castle. "It's unlocked," he informed me with a waggle of his brows.

I rolled my eyes and jumped out. Vito pulled away, the tyres crunching on the gravel. Taking a deep breath to calm my nerves, I pushed open the door, then turned around and locked it. Silence greeted me. The atmosphere was eerie, yet charged with energy. Or maybe that was just me. Soft lighting illuminated the clean lines of the kitchen, making it easy to see the bottle of Remy Martin with a crystal glass placed beside it. I grinned, picking up the note scrawled in Dav's handwriting.

Your second favourite drink...for courage. Your favourite is waiting...xx

I looked at the key. And knew exactly where. Picking up the ridiculously expensive bottle of brandy I splashed some in the glass, the aroma making my mouth water, but not as much as the thought of Dav waiting for me. Taking the bottle and the glass, I strode down the familiar corridor. From the old castle to the modern extension, this place felt like home now. Victor's house and coven was just a memory, one I deliberately pushed away until it was just a distant echo.

Striding steadily down the dark hallways, I made my way to the hidden door, thankful for my improved sight. Swallowing down some of the brandy, I smiled. Warmth spread through my insides. Dav knew me better than I knew myself. I had no idea what claiming a mate entailed, but I trusted him to guide me. Another swallow. My belly heated from the alcohol, but I was still starving. Clawing emptiness gripped me. I needed to feed. I needed Dav...

My boots echoed on the stone steps. I hadn't been down here since the day Dav had captured me, but I remembered everything about it, even the cell I'd been chained in. I wasn't sure why Dav wanted to do this down here, but I had an idea. I inhaled the scent of his excitement and lust. My whole body responded, my cock hardening and throbbing. Gods, the scent of his desire was a powerful aphrodisiac.

When I turned the first corner of the steps a soft flickering glow greeted me. Candles. I smiled. Who knew? My man was a closet romantic.

The closer I got, the stronger the scent of desire became. By the time I stepped through the open gate of the cell, I was shaking—my stomach cramping and my fangs long and ready.

My footsteps stumbled at the sight that greeted me.

"Gods above..." I whispered hoarsely, my erection jumping and nearly punching a hole through my combats.

Dav lifted his head, his fangs long, his eyes burning red and his cock hard and ready. The chains securing him to the wall were an exact replica of how I'd been chained that first day. His whole body tensed at my approach making the chains rattle.

"You're giving up control—to me?" My voice shook.

"Only for you."

His growled agreement set my blood on fire. I cupped his jaw with my hand, dragging my gaze over the chains and locks. "Who did this to you?" Jealousy squeezed my heart. Who'd seen him like this? Vulnerable and gloriously naked.

He smirked, remaining silent.

"Hm, I see." I smirked right back, sliding my hand down his body, brushing his cock lightly with my fingers. His hips punched forward, his groan music to my ears.

"Who, Dav?" My whisper was sultry, but I hated that it had probably been Vito.

"Oh...*gods*...Eli!"

I ran a finger over his slit and scooped up a bit of precum. Sucking it into my mouth, I smiled. "Tell me, Dav, or I'll not let you come. I'll drink your blood...but not let you mate with..."

I was lying through my teeth, but his reaction was more than worth it. Before I'd even finished speaking he blurted out, "The Count!"

I frowned. "But he was at the club when you left..."

Dav cocked his head and held my gaze. "Was he? He's old Elliot; dematerialising is easy for him."

"Right." But I wasn't interested anymore. They'd been together for hundreds of years. They would have seen each other naked plenty. I leaned forward and dragged my nose up his neck, inhaling deeply. "You smell of...need. Do you want me, Davlov Zoltar?" I pulled back until we were nose to nose, and I was staring deeply into his hungry gaze.

"More than anything in this world." His voice shook.

I fisted my hands, needing to touch him, but wanting to make him crazy with desire. "Forever?"

"Yes, yes, forever. You're *mine*." His growl was possessive, his breath coming in pants.

"Good, because you're mine, too, and I won't share you."

"Never. Now claim me. You have control over this, Elliot. Don't make me wait."

I smirked at his demand. "Oh, I'm definitely claiming you. But I think I'll have some fun first." I dropped to my knees before him and took his length in my fist, gripping until he was engorged and throbbing in my hold. I leant forward, my mouth almost touching his glorious cock, but not quite. I licked his tip with my tongue.

"Fuck, Elliot. Please!" Dav hissed, punching his hips forward towards my mouth.

I looked up at him. "Who's in control?"

"Ah, shit, you are." He panted heavily.

"That's right, baby. Now relax and enjoy." I twirled my tongue around his crown, enjoying his taste and the deep moans he made, but I wanted more. I glanced at his face, revelling at the raw pleasure I saw before I swallowed his length, working him with my hands and mouth, sucking and twisting until he was crying out. I explored his body with my other hand, cupping his balls, then sliding my hand back further as I sucked one, then the other into my mouth—before pulling away.

His chest heaved, a snarl exposing his fangs. His eyes were hungry and frantic as I stood and stepped back. Holding his gaze, I slowly undressed. I wanted to tease him, but my body had other ideas. Just as I stepped out of my combats, a cramp hit my belly and my own fangs punched down further. I leaned forward, my own breathing fast and erratic. I clamped my jaw. My control was slipping…

"Elliot?" Dav's voice pulled me from the pain.

"Bloodlust…" I managed to get out.

"El, look at me. You need to feed." Dav tilted his head to the side, baring his neck to me. "Fuck me while you drink. Claim me."

Nothing on this earth could stop me. I shot forward, grabbed his hair and mashed my naked body against his. The feel of his hard length pressed against mine sent my mind offline. I kissed him hard, our harsh breaths and desperate sounds mingling, our tongues duelling. I'd wanted to string this out, to make him desperate, but my control was done.

"Lube?" I managed to ask when I reluctantly released his mouth to gasp for air.

"Near my feet."

I bent and picked it up, lathering my fingers and cock in the slick gel before resuming our kiss. Sensation nearly sent me to my knees as I slid our cocks together. I kissed along his jaw and slid my other hand down. I forced aside my desperate need to feed and slid my hand over his balls, massaging them until he could barely hold still before sliding my fingers further back. His breathing came faster and harder.

"I don't need prep, I'll heal."

"Shut up, Dav. I won't hurt you. Not like that, anyway."

He groaned as my finger breached him and I moved it in and out, working with the slide of his hips as he rubbed urgently against my body. I slid another finger in, stretching him until the muscle resisted me less. Carefully, I slid another in, deliberately angling them to hit his prostate. He shuddered and cried out.

"Oh, shit! El, stop! Please...I need you. Please take me...claim me...now," he begged.

I gave a satisfied smile against his mouth, my whole body heating at his words. My erection throbbed, my skin was on fire, and the need to feel his blood on my tongue was so consuming I had no hope of resisting his pleas. I eyed the chains like they were my enemy. "How do I get these off you? I want your legs."

Dav yanked one leg free then the other. The old chain links snapped like twigs. I didn't have time to swoon over that show of strength. All I wanted was to be inside him. I thrust a hand into his hair and dragged my aching fangs along his jaw to the pulse in his neck. His legs went around me and his arm muscles strained against the chains as he helped hold his weight. I angled my hips, practically vibrating with need as I notched my crown at his entrance and pushed, holding myself back from thrusting into his heat like I wanted to. I withdrew before inching in further.

"Fuck me, you're tight," I managed to breathe.

"Good..." Dav breathed before thrusting himself down onto my cock.

"Dav..." I cried out in protest.

"I'm good," he rasped. "Now fucking move!"

I pulled out, meeting the smouldering desire in his eyes before I slammed back in. "Like this?"

"Yes!" he panted, his eyelids fluttering. "Harder."

I obliged, gripping his hips and setting a punishing pace. I wanted his hands on me, but I knew if he wanted to he could easily break those chains. He gifted me control, and I loved it. I'd never been in control of my life. But this? Dav had shifted the power to me. And it was amazing. I picked up the tempo and drove in hard, pounding against his body. Flesh slapped against flesh, our grunts and cries mixing.

"Fuck me, you feel so good."

"Made...for...you," he panted. "Only you."

I wrapped my hand in his hair and pulled, exposing the strong column of his neck. "Yes...you are. *Mine.*" I snarled, homing in on that pulsation under his skin. My fangs pierced his skin and blood hit my tongue. His taste exploded over my taste buds.

Oh gods...

I couldn't get enough. I sucked and swallowed, pounding into him until he yelled and clamped down on me. I kept drinking him as he shuddered and cried out my name, over and over, the hot jets of his cum hitting his chest and stomach. The sensations were too much. My orgasm exploded, ripping through my cells hard enough it felt as if my bones were shattering and remaking themselves. That intense pleasure went on and on until I saw stars. A yell barrelled up my throat, but I didn't release Dav's neck. I couldn't. I slowed my hips, letting us both recover a little before I could even think about letting him go. I carefully unlatched my teeth from him and then slowly pulled out of his body. But my cock was still hard, and desire rolled through me as I took his mouth in a searing kiss. He moaned, and I swallowed it down. He hadn't gone soft either. I pulled back, and he grinned.

"Bloodlust," he explained, tilting his head over. "Heal me."

I narrowed my gaze on those two puncture marks. "No.

You're mine." I licked up the rivulets of blood and dragged my tongue over the wounds only once.

"Baby, I really am. But..." He broke the chains that held his arms. "Now it's my turn."

My legs went weak as desire and endless hunger barrelled through me, but he grabbed me, kissing me hard. "I got you. Trust me, Elliot, I'll get you through this. I'll give you everything you need."

I nodded. "I know you will." I clung to him, unable to do anything else. I kissed his neck and jaw, running my hands over his big shoulders, only just aware of a cold wind hitting my skin. A moment later, the world tilted, and softness met my back as Dav's scent surrounded me. We were in his room. His weight on me was glorious, his lips on my skin driving me wild, his slick fingers working my body. But it didn't last long.

"I can't wait any longer," he growled.

I turned my head and exposed my neck. "Then take me. Claim me...please, I need you."

He chuckled at my plea and grabbed my legs; lifting them, he pushed slowly but firmly into my body. I grunted and breathed through the feeling of discomfort and fullness.

"Don't stop," I told him when he hesitated.

"I can't. You feel so fucking good," he huffed, rolling his hips.

The feel of his weight on top of me, his blood pumping through my veins as he fucked me, was overwhelming in the best possible way. He angled his hips and I instinctively moved with him. Excitement made me claw at his back as I anticipated what was about to happen. I leaned up and kissed the side of his mouth then scraped my teeth over his jaw before dropping my head back and exposing my neck.

I groaned as Dav's fang's punched deep. At his first draw I detonated, my whole body spasming. With each suck of his lips another shock of pleasure took me—until I screamed, my body on fire. Dav drove his hips home harder and harder, frantic and wild until his rhythm stuttered. Warmth emptied into my body

KAREN TOMLINSON

and he gave a strained roar, which stayed trapped in his throat. He was as reluctant to release his hold on me as I had been with him.

His pace slowed until he stopped. Breathing hard, he released my legs and unhooked his fangs from my skin, laving the wound once. Satisfaction burned in his gaze. He supported his weight on his elbows as he rested his forehead on mine.

"Wow," I breathed.

Davlov stared down at me, my own love reflected in his eyes. "Wow, indeed." He leaned down and kissed me tenderly before rolling the tip of his tongue around my fangs. "You're mine now. My mate. And you mean everything to me."

I swallowed the ache in my throat. It was overwhelming to know that his words were completely and utterly true.

"Sleep now," he said, slowly pulling from my body.

I didn't care about the after effects of our claiming, the mess, the soreness, nothing.

"You'll need it, love. 'Cause no one else is getting near you now. I'm the one who will feed you to get you through this part of your bloodlust."

Pleasure shuddered through me at the thought of taking his blood and his body again. I smiled sleepily. "I can't wait. This was perfect."

Dav smiled and kissed me languidly before he rolled onto his back and pulled me closer, half draping me across his body. I let my head relax onto his chest, my mate's scent surrounding me and his strength buzzing through my veins. I'd never felt so content or so *safe* in my entire life. And the best part? It was forever.

"I love you," I whispered against his skin.

"Good, 'cause I adore you. And you're stuck with me now."

EPILOGUE

 lliot

Six Months later

"I wish we'd had you on our side when that damned Rift from Hell opened," Vito said, as we strode up the gravel drive towards the castle.

I raised my brows. "Really? Why's that?"

Vito grinned and slapped my shoulder. "Because you've turned into a badass fighter, kid. Of course, it's all down to your training partner. You wouldn't be anywhere near as good without him."

I rolled my eyes. "Jesus, Vito, arrogant much?" But I was grinning. Dav was busy and had a job to do, one I'd told him I didn't want to interfere with. It wasn't possible for him to train with me everyday to improve my skills to the level the Count required of his security staff. Instead, he'd tasked Vito to be responsible for my combat training. The trouble was, the vamp was damned good at his job, and he knew it. Then again, that was Vito all over. Arrogant. Self-confident. And a good guy.

"Who? Me?" he asked.

I laughed at his innocent expression. "You're an idiot."

He grinned back.

We walked the rest of the way in companionable silence. Birds tweeted from the nearby trees and the moon lit our way. It was a warm summer night filled with the heady scent of flowers, and it was almost dawn. That meant Dav would be back from the Gambit with the Count and Sorcha. My stomach lurched with familiar excitement at the thought of seeing my mate. I smirked. I'd only seen him a few hours ago, but it felt like too long.

We'd spent the past months spending as much time as possible together, getting to know each other. I'd discovered a passion for learning the piano. I wasn't bad at it, but I wasn't good, either. At least, that's what I thought; Dav had thought otherwise, saying I had a natural talent that needed to be nurtured. He'd paid for lessons, and I'd loved every minute of them, working hard to make the most of his belief in me. But most of all I enjoyed playing just for him in the castle music room when I knew no one else was around. I touched the scar beneath my ear. The Count had removed Victor's rune, which to me had been like unlocking shackles and freeing me from my past. I had Dav's initials tattooed in vampire runes over my heart now. I touched the area and smiled. Some days I had to pinch myself to make sure my new life was real. I was happy, content in a way I hadn't thought possible. Physically, I was as big and strong as other vampires. My vampire side had all but swamped my human side now that I'd gone through bloodlust, and though I knew it was still there, I felt more vampire than anything.

Davlov and the Count agreed that my mother must have been from an ancient Original family and that my body and blood were almost entirely vampire now that I regularly fed from Davlov. I could still go out in daylight. Whether that was my human blood or Davlov's ancient blood, I didn't know, but it meant we could spend more time enjoying our lives together, exploring places and doing amazing things that I'd never had the opportunity to do before.

Vito and I were twenty feet from the door when the air shimmered, and a bright light exploded in a flurry of sparks. Wind sucked at my hair and legs, trying to unbalance me.

"What the fuck?" I yelled, reaching for the dagger on my thigh.

"It's a portal," bellowed Vito over the noise of the wind, slamming his hand over mine. "Put your weapon away."

I blinked. Hearing about portals from Davlov had not done this miracle of magic any justice. It was a spectacular sight.

Two males stepped from the portal. One was huge and so muscular that he looked like he could crush a car with his hand alone, and the other guy was stunning in the way only fae could be. He had the prettiest, bluest hair I'd ever seen.

I gaped, my footsteps halting.

"Shit, what are they doing here?" muttered Vito.

"Who are they?"

"The big one is Connor Rawson. He's King of the Shifters. And the other one is the Prince Heir, the ruler of Faerie while the King is in exile here on Earth."

"Shit, really?"

"Yeah. So stop gaping, and mind your manners, but don't show any fear or they'll never respect you."

The big guy glared at me. I felt an otherworldly power touch my skin before he nodded a greeting. "I'm looking for the Count. It's urgent."

I swallowed hard, but straightened my spine. I wasn't the same kid I'd been before I met Davlov. No matter how lethal and powerful, I would never cower from another person again.

I strode forward. "I'll take you to him." I looked them both in the eyes before I respectfully moved my gaze away.

Power emanated from the two as they walked behind me down the corridor towards the Count's office. I could feel the mate bond tug me forward, and it was a chore not to hurry. I knocked, but didn't stop. I doubted these two kings would appreciate standing outside Bal's office waiting for him to answer the door.

Davlov's scent hit me as I walked in, my eyes immediately finding his. He met my gaze but didn't smile, his attention immediately going to the two powerful immortals at my back.

"Connor? B'nar? What's wrong?" the Count asked, his colourless eyes searching their faces.

"I need your help. We have a problem." Connor pulled a phone from his jeans. Clicking the screen, he placed it on the table.

This is just for you, Shifter King. You allied with the wrong vampires. Break your alliance with Balthazar Rossi and the Originals who follow the vampire King and his son, or we will continue killing your kind until there are none left. I realise my brethren have failed to wipe out your Canadian pack—for now, but while they regroup, just sit back and enjoy the show."

Blood drained from my head. I wanted to throw up at the sound of that familiar voice. Staggering backwards, I leaned against the wall. It was that or fall. Davlov's gaze snapped to me, I could feel the weight of it even if I couldn't look at him.

I panted, my heavy breaths drowned out by the grunts and noise on the phone. It sounded like they were beating someone...

"Elliot?" Dav's voice was heavy with concern.

I took a deep breath and lifted my head. "I-I'm okay...I just..." but I couldn't get enough air in.

"Dav? Elliot? Is everything okay?" The Count's gaze shifted to me.

Two more powerful gazes swung my way. Sweat trickled down my spine, and my breaths came faster—until Dav took my face in his calloused hands. That touch. Everything. It grounded me.

"Breathe with me, baby. In...out...in...that's it...out...good." His chest rose and fell slowly and deeply and I mirrored his movements, gripping onto his large biceps with my shaking fingers. No one spoke until I'd calmed, and was breathing steadily again. The Count's eyes remained on me, but he didn't ask what had triggered my panic. He and Dav exchanged a look. Neither of them needed to. That voice was in my psyche as a trigger for every bit of pain and subjugation I'd suffered from being a little boy. I stayed propped against the wall with Dav's hands on my shoulders, and the Count moved his attention back to Connor, his face utterly cold.

"I'll come with you. Hunting them down by scent will be easy for me. But that fucker is mine."

"Thank you." Connor sounded relieved. "You can have him. I just want my brothers back alive. That pack were the ones who broke out of prison with me. I owe them."

"I understand," said Bal.

"B'nar will portal you there. I'll join you as quickly as I can with more reinforcements, but that fucker's threatened my home. I need to make sure there isn't an immediate threat to my mate and our baby."

The Count nodded. "Dav?"

Dav gave his boss a reassuring smile. "I've got it. I'll look after everything."

Bal nodded and glanced at the door, a line appearing on the bridge of his nose.

"Sorcha will be protected," Dav assured the Count, who nodded again, and I was sure I saw relief in the powerful vampire's eyes.

He walked over and laid a hand on Dav's shoulder.

"Thank you."

Dav swallowed. "No thanks necessary. Just get that bastard."

Bal looked down at me. "I promise."

The three males strode away, leaving Dav and me together.

"That *was* Victor, wasn't it?" Dav pulled me into his arms and held me tightly.

I wrapped my arms around him. "Yeah. He had an English accent, but it was definitely him. I'd know his voice anywhere."

He grunted, but didn't move. We stayed like that, wrapped in each other. Dav's scent filled my nostrils, and I let myself relax into my mate. I was safe here.

"If Bal's hunting him, we won't need to worry about revenge. He'll be dead before the moon rises again tomorrow."

"Will he?" I wasn't going to feel bad for hoping that was true. I'd known Victor was cruel, but the level of cruelty I'd just heard on that video sickened me.

"Yep, or as good as—Bal's prisoner."

I hugged my mate tightly. "Good." But nerves fizzed in my belly at the thought that Bal might bring Viktor back to the castle.

A crash of pans and a screeched expletive echoed deep in the castle.

Dav's chuckle mirrored my own. "She's burnt or dropped the dinner again."

"Yep, we'd better go and make sure she's still in one piece."

Hand in hand we sauntered down to the kitchen.

Sorcha darted a look at us as we entered before she quickly lowered her gaze, dropping to her knees to pick up the mess of cooked pasta off the floor.

"Do you need help?" asked Davlov, his voice coolly professional.

I squeezed his hand hard in warning. The poor girl seemed more anxious than ever. Probably because Bal had just left. I'd have to tell my mate not to mess with her so much. I recognised the signs of previous abuse, and though she tried not to show it, she was wary in Dav's presence. He would never hurt her, but she needed time to believe that. He shrugged at me, but relaxed his features a bit.

"N-no, I-I'm fine, Davlov," she stammered. "I just…the stupid pan's really heavy."

"Well, let me know if you do."

I rolled my eyes and detached my hand from Dav's, dropping to my knees. "Did you hurt yourself?"

"No," she whispered, biting her bottom lip.

"Good. Let's get this cleaned up then."

Smiling at her, I helped scoop up the pasta, shrugging when she gave me an unsure look. "It's okay. You can trust us, Sorcha. The Count might not be here, but you aren't alone. Let us know if you need anything. Okay?"

She nodded, looking a little less flustered. When the mess was cleaned up, we both stood.

"Thanks," she said, with a small smile.

"You're welcome. Remember, come and find us if you need anything."

"I will."

"Good. See you later," I said as Dav pulled on my hand leading me out of the door.

Side by side, we wandered through the dawn light towards our home. It was a new annex, built on the back of the castle. A mating present from the Count. It was gorgeous and I loved it. It was our own personal space. Dav had handed over responsibility for decorating it to me, and it had filled me with joy to choose the furnishings and all the little bits of homey stuff that made it uniquely ours.

"The war's escalating, isn't it?" I asked, dread dragging at my chest, making my heart heavy.

"Yeah. I'm afraid it is. Balthazar is the King's champion and advisor. He commands hundreds of thousands of vampires across the world, our kind and Mades. The King's own troops, together with Bal's, are enough to make anyone of any race think twice about trying to take the Blood Throne. Unless they're mad."

I frowned despite the emotion and sense of belonging in my chest at being classed as *his kind*. "Is this really all about the Blood Throne?"

Dav pulled me down onto the small bench outside our front door. We sat and watched the birds as they landed in the courtyard feeding on insects, and the scent of honeysuckle filled my nose.

"Who knows? But it is the seat of power for the Vampire King. Whoever sits on it has dominion over all vampires. Including the Mades who are still loyal. If vampires don't abide by the King's rules they die. Balthazar and I enforce that."

I smiled and leaned in to kiss his cheek. "Powerful as fuck, aren't you?" I teased.

Dav smirked, but his eyes remained serious. "El, Victor's threatened the most powerful shifter in existence. Connor's our ally, and we need the shifters and the fae on our side, no matter how powerful Balthazar is. If Bal's enemies can weaken him by any means, especially by alienating, or killing, his allies, it will mean bloodshed for everyone, not just the vampires. The fae and shifters are leaders in finance and technology. Our enemies have already started a financial war. They're closing banks that used to be sympathetic to vampires. They're stealing money off ancient Original families and using it to finance their war. They have technological capabilities far beyond ours, and are stealing and laundering money via electronic means. But most disturbing of all, they're turning humans against us by using the bloodlust virus to cause mass slaughter. We're strong, but if humans turn on supernaturals it will be a global slaughter on both sides. The only way out of this is to hunt down the ones who are fuelling this war and end them. Viktor's the first lead Bal's had in a long time."

"If Balthazar's so powerful, surely the war will be over quickly?"

"It's not that easy. We don't know who's leading them, or who their allies are. Whoever it is, is powerful and cunning." Dav leaned back, watching a bee as it went about its business, flying along a bed of dahlia's.

"But I don't understand. If they're already so powerful, why do they need to incite a war?"

Dav crossed his arms over his chest and contemplated the

clear blue sky. "From the beginning of time there's always been someone who craves more power, more strength, more money, more…everything. And Bal is ancient, one of the most omnipotent creatures in this world. That means he's always a target. More so when he's one of the only obstacles between their quest for power and the throne."

I contemplated Dav's beautiful profile. "Has he never wanted the throne for himself?"

Dav smiled. "No. Once he's given it, his loyalty is unwavering. When the royal family was slaughtered over a thousand years ago, he survived. It took him years, but he reinstated the king's bloodline and swore to protect it, and that's what he'll do until the day he dies."

"But he's immortal, isn't he?" I suppressed a shudder at the thought of how old Balthazar Rossi actually was.

Davlov huffed a chuckle. "What was it you said to me? Oh yeah, *as old as fuck*, wasn't it? Well, Balthazar's that old, and far more. It doesn't mean he's invincible. He'd be real fucking hard to kill, but everything that lives can die, if you know how to end it."

"Oh."

Dav's chuckle rumbled through me. "Don't ask, because I won't tell."

We sat in silence for a while, both caught up in our own thoughts.

I gave a start when he stood up and held out his hand. "Come, I have a surprise for you."

"You do?"

He just smiled, and cocked his head expectantly.

I rolled my eyes but placed my hand in his. Warm fingers curled around mine.

"Close your eyes."

I did, but my steps were sure. I knew my way through this house with my eyes closed, even without Dav's hand in mine. He'd kissed me, fucked me, and led me through these rooms enough that I'd never forget them. Besides, I trusted him with everything I was.

"Open them."

I did. And gasped.

"Oh. My. God. Davlov…" My shocked whisper faded as I slapped my hand over my mouth.

In the corner of the living room, near the open patio doors, was a Bosendorfer Opus 50 grand piano. Shaking, I approached the magnificent instrument and trailed my fingertips over the keys. "This is too much…"

Dav came up behind me and wrapped his arms around my waist. "Nothing is too much for you. Now…" He guided me over to the stool and pushed me gently down. "Play for me."

So I did, my heart overflowing with love for the mate who had shown me what happiness truly was.

The End

Please leave me a review on Amazon. Thanks! It really helps with visibility.

If you want to read more about The Count, Sorcha, and the shifter who turns their world upside down, then join my mailing list for a heads up on when Blood Lust: Book 1 in The Blood Throne series will be released. The series will be a dark and seductive M/M/F why choose romance, with intrigue, love, betrayal, and a whirlwind storyline that will keep you guessing and take your breath away.

In the meantime, find all my other books on my website, www.karentomlinson.com, on Amazon, and in hardback at other retailers.

For now, thanks for reading! I hope you've enjoyed Dav and Elliot's story!

Karen

ABOUT THE AUTHOR

Karen Tomlinson is a USA Today Bestselling author of action-packed, spicy romantic fantasy, and paranormal romance books.

Karen writes a mix of M/M, M/F, and M/M/F romance. If you love strong female leads, kickass heroines, swoon-worthy, powerful Alpha heroes, magic, action, battles, bloodshed, hot scenes, and a HEA (happy ever after) then look no further! Come and meet strong characters who will destroy worlds for those they love.

Like you, Karen adores books and likes nothing better than to lose herself in a spicy romance with amazing characters and a HEA! She lives in Derbyshire, England, (think Mr. Darcy territory) with her husband, twin girls, and her gorgeous dalmatian. As well as reading and writing books, she loves keeping fit, walking in the hills with her family, and dancing around with her earbuds in while singing badly!

You can find her books & current selling platforms on her website: http://karentomlinson.com

Or in her shop https://www.karentomlinson.com/shop

(Payment plan available)